Free Book

Receive a free copy of *Seeking Mr. Debonair: The Jane Austen Pact* at https://dl.bookfunnel.com/38lc5oht7r and signing up for Cami's newsletter.

Compromised

DELTA FAMILY ROMANCES #6

CAMI CHECKETTS

Birch River
PUBLISHING

Copyright

Compromised: Delta Family Romances #6

Copyright © 2022 by Cami Checketts

All rights reserved.

Chapter One

Melene Collier stayed close to her fourteen-year-old guide's back as they worked their way along the narrow path above the ocean. One wrong step and she'd plummet to the surf and the rocks a hundred feet below. Probably a death sentence, but she'd escaped so many death sentences over the years in her humanitarian work, what was one more?

Sorry, she said mentally to her guardian angels. *Not trying to make your job harder.*

Her Gramma Larue always claimed she made her guardian angels work overtime. Melene never meant to cause trouble or extra work for anyone, but her life of service was often "sketchy," as her younger sisters would say.

It was a semi-dark night with a pretty half-moon glinting off the smooth waves of the Baltic Sea. If she wasn't in such a precarious spot, she'd savor the beauty. She'd enjoyed the August nights near Poland's coastline as she worked with refugees from the conquered country of Banida, providing them food, shelter, and hope.

Her stomach churned. Hope was getting a little short as Commander Frederick had renamed himself King Frederick and was now setting his sights on Poland. Banida was a small country sandwiched between the northern ends of Germany and Poland. If Frederick had his way, Melene, the other volunteers, and these innocent people in desperate need and already displaced from their homes would be in the middle of a war zone. With no support and no escape.

The path turned inland from the ocean trail and they made their way through the thick forest. Visibility lessened and the trail became harder to follow. The tree canopy blocked out the moon's light and they didn't dare use a flashlight.

An at-risk family was heading their direction from Banida. Melene and Thomas were to assist the mom and her five small children to the relative safety of their camp while the husband went back to protect their home and farm and fight with the rebels still attempting to stand up to Frederick.

She shivered even though it wasn't cold. Frederick was evil clear through. The psychopath claimed he was a descendant of Frederick the Great and the rightful heir of all of Europe. He ruled with intimidation, threats, bribes, conspiracies, and murder. Melene had heard stories that would give grown men nightmares.

In Africa last year, she used to read Michael Vey books to the older children and teenagers at nights to help them with their English and to bond together. They all agreed Dr. Hatch was the most disturbing and evil villain imaginable, and she'd often skipped reading aloud the most sickening paragraphs of those books.

Sadly, the stories about "King" Frederick weren't fiction. It was all too reminiscent of Hitler's rise to power, and Melene prayed daily for the blameless people in danger and for the United Nations to pull their heads out of their rears before Frederick grew too strong to stop.

Thomas stopped so quickly that Melene ran into his bony back. He steadied her with his arm. They were far enough away from the ocean trail and in thick dense trees, so she wasn't in danger of falling off a cliff. Why had he stopped her?

Her ears perked up as she heard voices. The family they were searching for?

Two male voices carried through the trees, and she felt instantly disappointed and concerned. These two strong male voices were definitely not their misplaced refugees. One of them had a heavy European accent, possibly German, the other crisp tone was definitely British.

She froze and listened. The voices wouldn't project far through this dense foliage, which meant the men were less than twenty feet away. That was horrifying. She and Thomas had almost walked into two unknown men. As close as they were to the fighting, these could be rebels or Frederick's men. Either way, she and Thomas wouldn't be safe. Even the rebels whose families Melene and her associates were feeding and clothing might shoot first and ask questions later with how jumpy and outnumbered they were.

Should they backtrack?

The men weren't moving, and neither was Thomas. She imagined any movement from her or Thomas might be heard and investigated. She prayed she could keep the teenage boy safe and be impressed to know when to make their getaway. But what about their family? They couldn't desert them to whoever these men were.

The men shifted, and she held her breath and stayed still so they couldn't see or hear her. She could now clearly see the guy facing her as the man with his back to her held up a cell phone, showing him something on it. The man was tall and had sharp features, paler skin, and dark eyes and hair. He would probably be considered classically handsome, but Melene could see cruelty in his features. With all she'd seen and experienced in her charity work throughout the world, she'd come to recognize ruthlessness and steer far away from it.

She tugged on Thomas's arm, but he didn't move.

The man holding the phone explained slowly in accented English, "The yacht is *My Lady*. It leaves Marina Lubmin at nineteen hundred hours. Chancellor Kohl and staff on board. Your bombs must be set *before* it leaves."

Melene's eyes widened. They were planning to assassinate Germany's most powerful leader. These men had to be Frederick's. Would they take on Germany before Poland? Were the threats against Poland only a smoke screen? Was Frederick strong enough to fight on two fronts?

Melene would pass the information on and hope the right people could stop the assassination attempt. She shivered. What she and Thomas had just overheard was their death sentence if these men discovered them. She yearned to back away and tug Thomas with her, but she was afraid to make any noise.

"Do not presume to instruct me on my mission," the Brit sneered at the German in crisp, articulate tones. What was it about that voice? That face?

Her horror tripled and her body shook so hard she was afraid she'd hit into a tree branch. Melene recognized him. General Carl Phillip. She'd seen him on television, on the right hand of King Frederick. He'd defected from Britain's army and was now a hired mercenary who Frederick had appointed as one of his generals. Phillip was extremely wealthy, connected, and well-trained. He had a reputation as a cold-blooded killer and a womanizer who didn't take no for an answer.

Her pulse raced and ice pricked at her neck. What kind of nightmarish mess had they stumbled on to? How could she get Thomas to safety? She prayed desperately for some miracle that she and Thomas would stay safe and that their family wouldn't appear and blunder onto these men like they nearly had.

Against all she hoped and prayed, the two men started walking in their direction. Her stomach dropped. No, no, no! There was no chance the men wouldn't bump right into them on the path.

The man with the phone was groveling loudly his apologies and that of course the general was "the expert."

Thomas glanced back at her, the fear in his eyes palpable. "Run," he mouthed.

Melene nodded. It was run or the men would walk right into them. Melene could run fast, and so could Thomas. She often organized foot races with the youth to get them exercise and distract them. Thomas was one of the few who could beat her consistently.

But what if these men shot them in the backs?

They had no choice. Running was their only option, and she knew it. Melene pivoted and took off at a sprint. Thomas was so close to her backside that he clipped her heel. She stumbled and for a horrific moment, she was certain she'd hit the dirt. But heavenly hands seemed to balance her and she kept flying forward. She flung one foot in front of the other at the fastest pace she'd ever run, and she'd beaten state records back in high school.

Low curses came from behind and then the dreaded footsteps taking up pursuit. Melene maintained her pace through the moon-dappled forest. Thankfully, Thomas kept up and neither of them tripped or ran into a tree. The men weren't as fast, and she could sense them falling behind. That was the only good news of the night.

Would they shoot at them? She flinched just imagining them pulling their guns and taking aim. She'd been in many dangerous situations throughout the past few years, but a known murderer, the right-hand man of the most evil man currently on the planet, chasing her through a dark forest with a fourteen-year-old relying on her to save him, might top them all.

She burst out of the forest trail and almost flew off the ledge and to the rocks and ocean below them. Grabbing a tree branch, she whirled around and slid onto the ocean path. Thomas stayed right behind her. Her brain screamed at her to slow down so she didn't plunge off the cliff, but she'd risk splatting on the rocks over being caught by General Phillip.

Thomas panted for air behind her. They had no coverage now that they were out of the trees. The half-moon had seemed a blessing earlier, but now it felt like a curse. Out here on this ledge, the men could pick them off like ducks.

Luckily, no gunshots yet. Did that just mean the men knew they'd catch them eventually, and they wanted to know who they were and what she and Thomas had heard before they tortured and killed them? The men also hadn't yelled or called out to them. It was eerie. Especially as the thud of their heavier footsteps seemed to grow louder. Was it her fear that made their footfalls reverberate so loudly through her head?

All she knew was she could not afford to stop or slow down.

Melene had been dubbed "sunshine" and "sweetness" by children and their parents in different languages the world over. She felt like neither right now. "Horror" and "darkness" were all she could feel.

The trail split in front of her. Melene could stay on the ridge and run the half mile back to their camp. She and Thomas were faster, but the men would easily follow them and catch them when they reached camp.

More people might mean safety, but their camp had no military support or healthy men between the ages of fifteen and sixty. The men were either fighting with the rebels or they'd been killed or conscripted into Frederick's army. A ruthless leader like General Phillip might kill more than just her and Thomas if she led him to the refugee camp. She couldn't willingly put those people on that man's radar.

She squinted into the darkness and could make out the other trail. It led down through craggy rocks and to the beach and ocean. Choosing that direction looked to be a completely idiotic choice. If she remembered right, the beach wrapped around the cliffs and back to some restaurants, bars, and shops, but she wasn't certain if this was that spot. If it was an isolated beach, they could swim to get away, but more likely she would trap herself and Thomas. The men behind them would easily extract their information and then kill them. She knew her calling in life was risky, but she'd never been in mortal peril this deep, or worse, put a child in danger.

She said a prayer for direction and darted down toward the beach.

"Melene," Thomas hissed from behind her, obviously thinking it was the wrong choice. She half expected him to go the other direction, but he followed her.

Dumb, dumb, dumb. Why had she gone this way? Was she following inspiration or desperation? It was hard to know when she was terrified and running for her life.

She kept scrambling over rocks and down the steep trail, her speed significantly limited by the terrain. Almost halfway down, she let herself glance back.

The general appeared at the top of the trail, and his cohort stepped up next to him. The light of the moon glinted off the sharp planes of his face. He gave her a leering smile that made her skin crawl. This man was pure evil, and he was going to enjoy trapping and torturing her.

Chapter Two

Melene hurried down the precarious trail as fast as she could. Tripping over a rock, she went down hard, scraping her knees and palms on the uneven boulders. She cried out.

"Okay?" Thomas asked, helping her back to her feet.

No! She wasn't okay, and he wasn't going to be okay.

Please help, she begged anyone in heaven who had a spare minute. *Sorry Gramma Larue,* she also muttered in her head. Her grandmother was going to give her the tongue-lashing of her life when she saw her again. Would that be on this earth, or would Melene be killed tonight and have to dread what was coming from her grandmother until she joined her in heaven?

"Yep," she grunted, lying to Thomas as blood trickled down her knees.

The minor injury was the least of her concerns as she heard pebbles being dislodged from above. The two men had started picking their way down the steep trail.

Melene hurried as fast as she dared. General Phillip wasn't in a hurry. He thought he had them trapped, and he was probably the type who enjoyed toying with his prey and making them suffer before he mercilessly tortured and then killed them.

He was most likely right in assuming she was trapped, but Melene refused to give up. Pushing her terror aside, she knew she'd felt inspired to go this way. She had to trust in that. She would pray they could run along the beach and get lost in the restaurants or bars that would still be open around the other side of the cliff. Worst case, if the beach didn't continue around the bend like she was visualizing, they'd swim to escape him. She would focus her positivity and faith on living another day to serve and lift and give love. Most importantly, she had to keep Thomas alive.

If not, please let Grammy Larue forgive me for "getting' meself killed in them darn jungles."

She almost smiled thinking of her outspoken grandmother back home in Colorado. At least her family was safe back at home. On the hard days, that always helped her get through.

She scrambled down the trail and finally skirted around the last rock. Sinking in the thick sand, she plunged to the left, praying and praying for protection and an escape route. The cliffs rose around her, and she recognized instantly she'd made an idiotic, death-certificate-signed mistake.

This wasn't the beach that connected to the restaurants. It was a beautiful, sheltered cove. Probably paradise to anyone on a bright, sunny day. At least to someone who wasn't being hunted and hadn't just trapped themselves and an innocent boy with a homicidal British maniac and his companion.

Glancing back, she could see General Phillip easing down the last half of the incline. He caught her gaze on him and gave her a wink and a grin. Her stomach churned. He was mocking her. It was obvious he enjoyed the terror he was inspiring.

"Thomas," she hissed, untying and ripping off her shoes. "We have to swim. It's our only chance."

"I no swim," he said, shaking his head, his dark eyes wide with fear.

Ah, no. Thomas was from a mountainous village and hadn't even seen the ocean before coming to their refugee camp. Why had she stupidly assumed any fourteen-year-old boy would know how to swim? Didn't they have lakes in their mountains? The Delta family from back home had a lake in their valley and her friend Aiden Delta had improved her and her friends' swimming skills in the chilly waters. Most of them had just wanted to see Aiden without his shirt on, but she'd actually listened to his tips and he'd helped her swim even better than the swim instructors of her youth. She could picture Aiden now with his irresistible smile and piercing blue eyes. He was far too good-looking just like all of the Deltas, but fun to tease and laugh with.

She blinked away the memory from home. Facing death was making her pensive.

"I'll tow you," she encouraged, grabbing his hand and yanking him toward the water.

Thomas looked as terrified of going into the ocean as he did facing the men. But he obediently slid his shoes off and let her pull him across the beach and into the softly breaking waves. The water was cool and welcoming, as if the ocean was offering them refuge.

"Stop."

The cold command and cocking of two pistols came from behind them. Melene had the impression nobody argued with that man, and she could only imagine he was accurate with his instruments of death.

Melene and Thomas whirled to face the men. They were at the bottom of the rocks, not stepping onto the beach, as if the sand would sully their boots. They each held pistols in their hands, pointed right at Thomas. How did they instinctively know she would protect Thomas?

Melene's pulse raced out of control. Could they dive into the water and swim away without getting shot? If they could both swim, they had a one in a million chance. With her pulling and towing a boy afraid of the water, they were dead.

She prayed desperately for some help or inspiration. With no idea what to pray for, she simply repeated in her mind, *Please, please, please help ... somehow.*

Thomas bravely splashed in front of her in the knee-deep water and put his hands out. "No kill the lady," he yelled.

General Phillip let out a cultured laugh that was echoed by the other man's more guttural chuckle. Their laughter cut off abruptly, as if they'd cued it. The only sound was the lapping of the waves and all of their panting breaths.

"It will be with pleasure that I shoot both of you between the eyes," General Phillip said, as if telling them he was going to eat a fillet of salmon for dinner. He made no move to step closer, knowing they had no escape. "After you explain precisely who you are, how you knew to eavesdrop on us, and what exactly you overheard."

"Why would we tell you anything if you're going to kill us?"

Melene hurled at him, stepping to Thomas's side despite his attempts to stay in front of her. There was no hope of escape. Despair stronger than the darkest night surged in her chest. Could she protect Thomas? Not if he couldn't swim.

"An American?" General Phillip's brows rose.

With Melene's mixed heritage of an Italian mom and African-American dad, many people had a hard time guessing her nationality, especially as she'd lived abroad for over ten years and had picked up muted accents from everywhere. Interesting that this man instantly knew she was American.

"Yes," she said, tilting her chin up. "I have American military protection, and you will be swiftly brought to justice if you murder us."

He laughed again. It was dark and cold. "Come now, my cheeky and lovely American. We both know your President isn't willing to rock the boat and risk nuclear winter. There might be a few military special ops units hoping to sneak into the action, but they have no jurisdiction here and wouldn't risk an international incident for a citizen who stuck her pretty nose in business where it does not belong. Your life is of little consequence to your military or your country." He looked her over, and her unease battled with the despair. "But you are an extremely beautiful woman. You want a deal, love? Everybody likes a deal when they're facing death." He nodded as if she were agreeing.

"No, thank you," Melene said primly.

"No touch Melene!" Thomas yelled in support. It sickened her that at such a young age, he instantly knew what the general was after.

"You haven't even entertained my offer." He didn't give them a chance to respond but went on, "I will keep you near my side, beautiful American, as long as I continue to fancy you"—he licked his lips—"and as long as you are only cheeky in the appropriate moments." He smiled. "And I won't even kill the boy."

Melene sucked in a breath. The thought of going anywhere near this man made her skin crawl, but if he'd truly spare Thomas, she would give herself up and pray somehow she'd be rescued before he ... she couldn't think about *that*. And who in the world could rescue her from the likes of this monster?

"I will have to cut his tongue out," General Phillip explained casually, "to make certain he squeaks to no one what he saw or heard tonight."

"No!" Melene cried out.

General Phillip lifted his left palm up in a sign of peace. His right hand still clutched the pistol aimed at them, so his sign of peace was a little hypocritical. "It is a very generous offer for a couple of spies."

"We no spies," Thomas spit out. "Melene protects and loves the children."

"How very benevolent of her," General Phillip said in what he probably thought was a charming voice. "Now she will have the privilege of loving me."

Melene's stomach curdled like she'd guzzled a gallon of rancid milk. She grasped Thomas's hand and prayed desperately. Was there any other option? She couldn't see one. The ocean waves lapped softly against the back of her legs, but sadly there was no refuge or reprieve there or anywhere. Not for her.

Tilting her chin up, she faked a bravado she didn't feel and said, "I will go with you."

"No!" Thomas yelled. "No!"

Phillip ignored the boy and smiled. His gaze traveled over her possessively. Her palms were clammy and she was going to spew. She couldn't believe she'd just agreed to subject herself to a life of purgatory, but for Thomas she would force her legs to walk across this sand and somehow survive the horror now in store for her.

"But you will not cut Thomas's tongue out," she continued in as level a voice as she could manage. "He is a staunch Catholic and will keep his word. He will swear to us by heaven above that he will not breathe one word of what happened to me or what he overheard, and you can trust that he will not."

Thomas stared at her as if she were insane. The look on the men's faces echoed it. Not even Thomas believed his promise to a devil like General Phillip was going to stick. As brave as this kid was, he might even tell the general to cut his tongue out. He could still write what had happened, but she didn't want to point that out.

Despair coursed through her. She was going to become this despicable man's property and Thomas would lose his tongue. It was all too gruesome to imagine. She'd been in many a bad or awkward spot, but nothing as desperate as this.

She could swear she heard low voices on the water and almost turned to look. Listening harder, despair filled her. There was nothing. No help. If anyone was out there, they were probably too far away to help or were smart enough to save themselves. Who could possibly save her or Thomas from the very devil himself.

Nothing but the soft waves offered support. General Phillip looked her over as if he already owned her, a disgusting smile on his lips. "I'm sorry, love, but you are in no position to make demands."

Melene knew he was right. She prayed desperately as she tried to think of some solution or answer. Slow, horrifying seconds ticked by. General Phillip's creepy smile grew, and her stomach tried to claw its way out of her throat. Her body shook. She tried not to picture what was coming, but the icy fear trailing across her skin felt like his foul hands were already binding her to him.

A soft splash sounded nearby, and she turned to look.

Melene was certain she was hallucinating. A shape rose out of the water only a few feet behind her. No one said anything as they all stared in shock. It was a man. A man dressed in a black scuba diving suit complete with a tank on his back, a face mask, a diving belt with weights, a knife, and a gun on it, and a ventilator in his mouth.

He pulled the ventilator out and grinned at her, water sparkling off his handsome face and hair. "Hi, Melene."

Melene couldn't for the life of her fathom how Aiden Delta, her high school swimming buddy and now an accomplished Navy SEAL, had just materialized out of the ocean like Aquaman at the exact moment she needed a knight in shining ... scuba gear.

"Aiden?" she whispered.

His blue eyes twinkled from behind the mask. "In a bit of trouble, are we?"

Her own eyes widened. She'd temporarily forgotten about the men ready to kidnap her and cut out Thomas's tongue. She whirled around and General Phillip and his buddy were now edging across the sand toward them.

"I'd suggest you stop and put down the guns," Aiden said to

them, lifting his goggles up onto his forehead so she could see his handsome face better. How in the world had he come up out of the water like he was Aquaman?

General Phillip chuckled. "You've lost the plot. Who is going to stop me ... you? A barmy git and all by yourself?"

Aiden gestured casually behind him. "My *mates*," he said, mimicking Phillip's accent. "You don't want to mess with any of us, you mangy twit."

Melene was terrified that Aiden had lost his mind and just signed his own death sentence trying to bluff his way into rescuing her and throwing British slang in to tick General Phillip off even more. Aiden had always been an overconfident tease and she wouldn't put it past him to bluff his way through a situation like this.

Suddenly dark shapes started rising out of the ocean, four— no, five—men, and they all had guns in their hands. A sleek boat cruised around the side of the cliff. Two men manned it. One was in the driver's seat, and the other one stood at the bow lofting a huge automatic-looking gun right at the general.

"Is it your hour to die, General Phillip?" Aiden asked. "Or would you like to head back up that trail and continue your evil deeds for a few more days?"

General Phillip glowered at them. "You Americans have no rights and no presence that is accepted here. You try anything and it will be the spark that annihilates millions of Americans ... in an instant."

He paused on his threat and Melene's horror of what might be coming grew. There'd been rumors King Frederick had amassed nuclear weapons, but she'd prayed they were just rumors. Aiden would have to swim away from her if him rescuing her or shooting General Phillip could cause the end of America.

Aiden and his men didn't so much as blink.

General Phillip's mouth tightened. "I have eyes and ears everywhere on this earth. I will hunt all of you down, slit your barmy throats, and take the woman as my prize."

"That was a lovely and inspiring speech. You're finished. Correct?" Aiden's gaze turned steely. "Right now, I'd suggest you set your guns down and slither back up the mountain like the snakes you are. I'd happily cause an international incident to rid the world of a slime-ball like you."

The man didn't move, and Melene had the awful feeling that Aiden couldn't actually kill or apprehend him without starting World War III and unleashing nuclear weapons on America.

If she and Thomas edged back to Aiden in the water, could he at least take them away? Fear clawed at her even with her rescuer this close, looking so brave and tough, but somehow unable to rescue her.

A gun fired and the sand next to General Phillip exploded, showering crystals of sand on him and his man.

Melene jumped and cried out, Thomas cheered, and the German man cursed. None of the men in the water made so much as a squeak. Melene had no idea who had fired. She prayed desperately the general would listen to Aiden and leave. Her heart beat so high and fast she couldn't swallow and hoped she wouldn't be called upon to talk.

General Phillip's gaze was full of rage, but to her surprise he slowly set his gun down. The other man followed suit. They backed toward the rocks. Melene panted for air. Would he really just leave? Would he bomb America?

He pointed a finger at Aiden. "I will find you ... squid."

Aiden tilted his head, all the teasing he usually displayed gone from his face. "You know, it's humorous when the Army or Air Force guys throw that term at us, but I don't like it coming out of your mouth." He pulled a knife from his belt, then flipped it open and pointed it at the general. "Maybe your tongue is the one that needs to be cut out. Then nobody would have to be subject to your vile, filthy lies any longer."

The general's eyes widened at the threat and suddenly he was hurrying up the mountainside.

Aiden winked at Melene, closed the knife, and fastened it back on his diving belt. "Bullies never like a taste of their own medicine." He lowered his voice. "Let's go. He won't give us much lead time and sadly, the pathetic worm wasn't bluffing about his power or his connections."

Melene was shaking with the fear of what could've been, but if she understood Aiden correctly, General Phillip would track them down, and he would bring an army next time.

Aiden pushed through the water to her and wrapped an arm around her waist. The warm pressure of him close somehow dispelled the fear and the darkness. She felt a sense of home she rarely experienced. She looked up into his handsome face and breathed out, "Thank you."

She wanted to gush about him being a hero and if she were being honest, she'd love to give him a kiss of gratitude, but she and Aiden weren't romantically involved and she could still feel the danger pulsing outside the circle of Aiden's arms. Sadly, there was no time to gush over him, catch up on family back home, or see if the spark crackling between them could go somewhere with this incredible Navy SEAL who'd just saved her from a fate worse than death.

There might never be time for any of that. General Phillip would be back, and he'd fulfill his threats. If they were lucky, he wouldn't unleash nuclear weapons on America.

She shuddered and clung to Aiden as they made their way to the boat. The water embraced her as surely as his arms. Aquaman had come for her. Could he keep her safe, or had she signed his death sentence and her own?

Chapter Three

The next twelve hours went by in a rush of interrogations, discussions, and chastisements. Aiden had been in the military long enough to not let any of it bother him. He answered each question honestly, and he kept praying the Navy would take the threat to Melene seriously. General Carl Phillip was a sneaky devil, and he hadn't been lying that he had connections all over the world. Where would Melene be safe?

If only Aiden could've shot him between the eyes, but that would've definitely caused an international incident. Bullets could be traced, and an unsanctioned hit like that would somehow get out. They always seemed to. Nobody knew if Frederick truly had nuclear weapons or if it was all rumors and bluff. America currently wasn't willing to find out.

Aiden and his SEAL Team 8 had been diving near the coast last night, mostly in a training exercise, but they were all open to the gift of any intel they secured so close to the war zone. They weren't supposed to be anywhere near here, but the sub they'd boarded a few days ago was quietly patrolling the Baltic Sea and the Banida and Frederick situation. All of them were hoping or praying, depending on their religious affiliations, that they would be allowed to help fight against the pathetic bully "King" Frederick and stop the atrocities he was committing. Finally, the Skipper had agreed to allow the elite SEAL team out to get a closer look. Aiden and his team had finished their dive and been ready to load into their small boat to head back to the sub when Jace, their CO who'd stayed in the boat, quietly told them he'd seen a woman and teenage boy running from two grown men. They'd slid back under the water and moved quick.

They probably shouldn't have intervened, but Aiden would do it again in a second. The fact that it was Melene Collier they had rescued still stunned him and had him saying prayers of gratitude every time he thought about it. The exotic beauty from their hometown of Summit Valley, Colorado, probably had more world experience than Aiden did. She'd traveled the world on one humanitarian mission or another for the past ten years. He hoped she'd never been in danger like last night, but he wouldn't doubt it. To think that scum General Phillip had almost kidnapped her and added her to his harem of women. Aiden's hand balled into a fist.

Melene's and Thomas's information had been passed on and prevented the German Chancellor from being murdered as well as made everyone realize Frederick's immediate plans were not only focused on conquering Poland. That helped ease a little of the pressure of a Navy SEAL team intervening where they didn't have permission and truly weren't supposed to be anywhere near this mess.

The Skipper, Executive Officer, and Chief of the Boat had been meeting with Jace to determine where they should take Melene to ensure her safety from General Phillip and his henchmen. They also had to decide what to do with Thomas. It was one thing to offer protection to an American citizen but quite another to harbor a refugee from a war-torn country that the U.S. wasn't an ally to.

Political crap like this ticked him off. All he wanted was Melene and the boy safe. He'd love to get her home to her family. He could ask his family to protect her. They were more than capable, but that might be exposure for the Delta secret that they couldn't afford right now. Having only recently defected from the British military, General Phillip would have many American associates and may have already heard whispers about the Delta "weapon," as those who'd tried to come after it recently called it.

Jace had overheard, and shared with Aiden, that General Phillip had already sent mercenaries to search the refugee camp for Melene and Thomas. They'd injured and threatened quite a few people but hadn't killed anyone. That was lucky, and surprising. Apparently, they wanted information about who Melene was, where she was from, and how they could find her. The threats and beatings were to warn them what would happen, and worse, if Melene and her little friend weren't turned over to them.

Aiden hit his clenched fist against his leg. He and Melene were only friends, but he felt fiercely protective of her. General Phillip would *never* find Melene and subject her to his filth . Not while Aiden was still breathing. But how could he protect her? He couldn't leave his team, and she couldn't travel around with a bunch of Navy SEALs.

He'd shot a message off to his grandfather late last night. Papa Delta would figure something out to help Melene. They had suspicions that King Frederick was after the Delta secret that Aiden's grandfather and family had been tasked with protecting. They would all do everything in their power to keep the secret safe from the likes of Frederick and Phillip and their evil cronies.

Watching over Melene could play into that, but the secret and Melene might be easier to guard in separate locations. He wondered at what point Papa would call him home to protect the secret full-time and retire from active duty. Papa had explained that he wouldn't be Secret Keeper—too obvious with his training and expertise—but he still felt the responsibility to protect his family and the secret deeply. He loved his family, but he hated the thought of settling down in the mountains and not traveling and engaging in training and combat. From what his family had been through lately, he supposed he would get plenty of combat and they were always training, but Aiden loved the travel and excitement and the ocean was his home. He'd wither and dry up without his salty seas.

A rap on his bunkroom door yanked him to his feet and across the small room. He all but ripped the door open.

"Lieutenant." A young enlisted man saluted him. "The Skipper would like a word, sir."

"Of course." Aiden hurried after the kid, grateful he'd showered and dressed and been awaiting this command. He was led down a hall, up a flight of metal stairs, down another hall, and into a conference room of sorts. No area was too spacious on a submarine, but the table could easily seat twelve and there was room for visual displays on one wall.

Melene was across the table, seated next to the Chief of the Boat. Aiden almost forgot to salute and come to attention when her big, dark eyes focused in on him, her full lips turned up in a welcoming smile, and her exotically beautiful face seemed to sparkle at his presence. Was it just the warmth of someone from home, or was Melene unique and the most gorgeous woman he'd ever seen? Did she look a little pale and exhausted? Anyone would after what she'd been through.

He saluted everyone and waited. The Skipper, commanding officer on this submarine, said, "At ease, Lieutenant. Would you like to inquire anything of Miss Collier?"

Aiden wasn't even aware the man had a personality, but he caught the mischievous smirk on the man's face.

"Yes, sir. Thank you, sir." He rushed around the table and Melene hurried to stand. He resisted the urge to pull her close but took the hand she offered, loving the warmth of her smaller and infinitely softer hand in his. "You're all right?"

"Thanks to you. I was terrified, Aiden, and praying so hard for a miracle. I didn't even know what to hope for or expect, but I was pretty certain we were dead. Then you and your men show up like angels from the ocean. Like Aquaman. Only more handsome." She winked and Aiden didn't know the last time he'd blushed, but he was right now. His cousin Maddie had informed him that as a SEAL he should embrace the Aquaman reference, as Jason Momoa was "extraordinarily hot and appealing."

A throat cleared. "*My* men actually rescued you," Jace, his CO and close friend corrected. He brushed a hand through his short blond hair. "Thank you for saying how handsome and angelic we are."

"Oh, excuse me." Melene shared a look with Aiden that made his stomach do an interesting somersault, then she focused on Jace and nodded. "Thank you, sir, for allowing the handsome and angelic Aiden Delta, aka Aquaman, to rescue Thomas and me."

Jace gave Aiden a long-suffering sigh and rolled his eyes. "Always the hero with the women, aren't you?"

"Someone's gotta be." Aiden gave his devil-may-care grin to his friend, but he didn't like the way Melene's smile dimmed at Jace's comment and his response.

The Executive Officer clearly didn't think they needed to waste time with all this banter. Jace and Aiden would've just been getting started. Especially with a fun, beautiful lady like Melene around to tease with. You could always tell how long an officer had been in the office and out of the field by if they still understood the need for banter and dark humor.

"You've created quite the mess, Lieutenant." He pointed at a chair next to Melene.

Aiden sat straight in the chair and faced the men. "General Carl Phillip created the mess. We were just evening the score a bit."

"Whatever you want to call it, thank your lucky stars you're related to Admiral Davidson Delta." The XO said his grandfather's name with the utmost respect. Aiden's neck prickled. He tried not to call in favors based on his grandfather's reputation, but he sure would pull that card to get Melene safely back home. He already had by reaching out to his grandfather.

"You've been assigned on a special mission, Lieutenant," the Skipper said.

Aiden looked at Jace. He nodded slightly, though his bluish-gray eyes showed he didn't appreciate losing a member of his team for an undefined amount of time. Especially if war was on the horizon.

Aiden hated the thought of leaving his team, brothers almost as close to him as the four blood-related ones he'd left in America, but he could only assume the "special mission" meant getting Melene home and far from General Phillip's reach. His shoulders tightened, remembering how the man had looked at Melene and his threat that he would find her.

"You and Miss Collier will move from ship to ship until you are deposited at an unnamed location in the Caribbean where you will hide until General Phillip tires of his quest to acquire Miss Collier."

"Hopefully gets distracted by his next beautiful target," the Chief of the Boat put in.

Acquire? Nobody was acquiring Melene. She wasn't just some beauty, though he couldn't claim she wasn't exquisitely beautiful, but Melene had depth, character, grit, and the most charitable nature he'd ever known.

The muscles bunched in Aiden's neck and he wished he would've just pummeled and then drowned that loser General Carl Phillip when he had him in his grasp. Sure, it could've become an international incident, but it would've saved a lot of misery for a lot of people. Melene included. Aiden would've happily taken the wrath for it.

"You have been informed that Phillip has a million-dollar bounty on her head?" the Chief of the Boat asked. "Only payable if she's alive and uninjured."

Melene sucked in a breath next to him.

Aiden had the craziest feeling that he should take her hand in his and reassure her that loser would never get close to her again. Of course he refrained.

"I wasn't aware of that, sir," Aiden said.

The Chief of the Boat looked as disturbed as Aiden felt. "Admiral Delta has arranged everything and I'm sure you two will be very comfortable. When the bounty is removed, as I'm assuming it will be soon—Phillip is smart enough to know he should concentrate his time and money on his leader's agenda and not his own—you will escort Miss Collier back to Colorado, where she will stay, and you will return to active duty."

"Excuse me, sir, but I am not one of your sailors," Melene said, her voice dripping with sweetness. Aiden was glad it wasn't him who'd made the comment. "I am a manager for Health for All, and when the danger has passed, I will also 'return to active duty.'" She smiled so beautifully Aiden didn't know how anyone would tell her no. He was so impressed by her bravery, but terrified that she'd get hurt or killed one day. Especially if General Phillip survived this war of Banida's and gained more clout, money, and authority. The man was brilliant, ruthless, and powerful. And no matter what the Chief of the Boat said, Melene would be impossible to forget, and Phillip might always have a barbed hook angling for her.

The Chief of the Boat stiffened and looked at the Skipper. The Skipper appraised her and said solemnly, "Miss Collier. You are correct that we are not your commanding officers. I only hope you think of your own safety and the family who loves you back home before you decide to assume another position in an uncontrollable environment." His voice dropped and his gaze became penetrating. "Besides the usual dangers to a beautiful American woman, you have an added layer of being a target of General Carl Phillip. The man has proven to be sneaky, well-connected, well-funded, smart, and he loves to coerce women who are ... a challenge."

Melene's face tightened, and once again Aiden wanted to reach for her hand. He would protect her. But what about after he returned to active duty and she doggedly insisted on returning to her charity work? Could her family talk her out of going back? Was that fair to her? Aiden tried to change the world by using his well-honed fighting skills to right wrongs and protect those in danger. Melene changed the world by loving, teaching, and empowering the motherless and the oppressed. She was incredible. And he couldn't stand the thought of her in danger like she'd been in last night. Next time, he and his buddies would most likely not be there.

"We can't force you back to America, but I would plead with you to think of one other thing besides your family and your own safety. You prayed for help in that cove and Commanding Officer Pitcher, Lieutenant Delta, and six other men came to your rescue. What if they or someone who's willing and able to fight for you don't miraculously show up next time? What if you had the opposite odds and our SEALs were outnumbered four to one and you got those eight elite men killed?" He stared her down.

Aiden and Jace exchanged a look. If the four to one comment had been from anyone closer to their rank level, they would've asked for an actual challenge. They both held their tongues out of respect.

"Something to think about," the Skipper said. "Meeting is adjourned. Get these two on a submersible to the *U.S.S. Bravado.*"

The Skipper stood, which meant all the men in the room stood as well. At attention.

"What about Thomas?" Melene asked, rising out of her seat and pinning the Skipper with a determined gaze.

Aiden had always liked and admired Melene. She was sweet, beautiful, smart, and fun to talk to, but his estimation of her kept rising. Of course she would make sure the boy was taken care of.

The Skipper looked to the XO. "We've assigned a team to escort the boy to a refugee camp in Texas where he'll be far from General Phillip's reach. He might not have a price on his head like you do, but he's in a significant amount of danger."

Melene grasped Aiden's arm. He didn't know if she even realized she'd reached for him. She didn't look at him but was focused on the XO. "But his family. Will they even know what happened to him? Will they ever see him again?" Her voice was full of horror.

It was interesting that she'd been so brave about herself being in danger and possibly never seeing her family again, but the boy being taken from his family about undid her. Aiden felt sympathetic for the boy, but his family would probably want him to live through puberty. If Thomas went back to that camp in Poland, Phillip would have him murdered by week's end. They could only hope the general wouldn't kill his family and others in the camp when they returned and found no new information on Melene or Thomas.

"I think his family would prefer he lived," the Executive

Officer said, not unkindly but definitely matter-of-factly. "We can pray this war gets resolved and they can be reunited."

Melene jutted out her chin. "I will pray desperately for that."

The Skipper gave her a nod of respect. "As will we."

The three men each nodded to Melene. Jace and Aiden saluted as they strode from the room.

"At ease," Melene said sweetly as the door shut.

Aiden relaxed and smiled at her. "I remember you being a tease, but not quite so feisty."

"Feisty?" Jace whistled. "I thought the Skipper was going to court martial a civilian when you didn't bow to his very thoughtful demands."

Melene lifted her eyebrows. "Let him try. I hate when people try to tell me I can't serve the children and I'm putting myself in danger."

"Noted," Aiden said, understanding why she'd feel that way, but also wondering if she shouldn't listen to solid and valuable advice. There were other ways to serve children besides putting yourself in extreme danger. He almost smiled at that thought. He was in extreme danger every day, but he'd been expertly trained from birth on up how to deal with intense situations.

"Well." He smiled at Melene. "Are you ready to ride in a submersible?"

"I have no clue what that is."

"You're in for a treat. You don't get seasick in small crafts, do you?"

"Violently," she said, smiling happily at him.

Jace chuckled. "I hope you're teasing."

She shrugged, giving nothing away.

"How are you feeling right now?"

"Dizzy, swallowing down bile, and my stomach is moving like a parkour expert."

Aiden's eyes widened. Seasick. That's why she looked so tired. Ah, dang. The next few days were going to be rough for her.

Jace whistled. "You're pretty impressive not to complain."

She *was* impressive, and Aiden didn't like Jace noticing. He should've laughed at himself. Any unattached male, and sadly a lot of attached ones, would notice how impressive, sweet, loving, and beautiful Melene was. Jace was still healing from his wife deserting him a year ago. Aiden should be grateful his friend could be distracted by Melene. Somehow he wasn't.

"I'd complain, but nobody would listen." Her full lips smiled teasingly at Jace.

They all laughed, but Aiden thought it was time to get her away from his CO and closest friend outside his family. "We'll go visit the medics on our way to pack." Aiden took her arm, liking the feel of her warm, firm flesh against his palm.

"I have nothing to pack." A small frown appeared on her beautiful lips, and Aiden had the completely irrational desire to kiss it away.

He had to stop with thoughts like that. He was on an assignment. As soon as he was done, he'd go back to active duty and Melene would go back to her charity work, unless she listened to the Skipper's advice and went home to her family.

They had no future. Even if Aiden had been into meaningless dating, Melene was not the type of girl you dated and left behind. She was the unicorn, wife material, the perfect mix of sweet and a little sass, humor and intelligence, beauty and Christian light.

He forced a smile. "We'll find you clothes and toiletries some-where." Actually, he'd text Papa and make sure wherever they were going was stocked with everything Melene might need.

"Thank you." She gifted him with that beautiful smile and his stomach pitched happily. He never got seasick, so he couldn't attribute his stomach's movement to that.

Jace gave him a look over Melene's head. His friend was jealous of his assignment, but also commiserated. It would never work to fall for an innocent, charitable beauty like Melene. Jace had tried love and marriage, and had gotten burned in the worst way. Aiden had seen the devastation his friend dealt with. Melene was off limits for his heart's safety and her own.

She stumbled as the sub swayed. Even deep under the ocean, there were currents. Aiden wrapped his arm around her, and his pulse took off like he was in a swim competition. The pressure of her beautiful form close was too tempting. He had to keep reminding himself Melene wasn't a date but a protection detail.

She smiled up at him, and the ship seemed to tilt on its side.

Aiden had to stay strong. Even though doing so with tempta-tion like Melene this close may be harder than not ringing the bell in BUD/S training.

Off limits, he repeated sternly to himself.

This sweetheart was definitely off limits to a salty dog like him.

Chapter Four

Melene was grateful to Lieutenant Aiden Delta for a multitude of reasons, starting with him miraculously saving her life, but the pressing reason right now was that over the last seventy-four hours —she thought that's how long Aiden had said they'd been traveling—he'd kept her eating saltines, sipping water, taking motion sickness pills, holding her hair out of the way when she puked, getting her to the "head" as they called it for a shower or to brush her teeth, and cleaning up her vomit while she was gone.

Miraculously, they'd made it off their final ship transfer. She'd stopped counting how many times she'd thrown up and simply focused on Aiden's solid presence that never left her side. There was a comfort, protection, and sense of home the highly accomplished yet compassionate SEAL exuded that she wanted to cling to. She wondered how she'd made it through the last ten years without him. It was probably just the dehydration and lack of sustenance that made her so needy, but Aiden didn't seem to mind.

She should be humiliated that she'd sullied her last set of clean clothes, hadn't had time to take a shower before they left the last large ship, had forgotten her toothbrush and military-issued toiletry kit on the same ship, and Aiden had seen her at her lowest point in years.

She was usually the strong one. The person who took care of others. But as much as she loved to swim in the ocean, she'd never done well on the rocky seas and usually avoided traveling by boat. She'd lost track of how many ships, some of them "submersibles" that were worse for her sea sickness because of no fresh air, they'd been on. The larger battle cruisers and submarines were okay but still not completely free of rocking or swaying if they were above the sea and strong ocean currents if they were below. She never settled completely before they were transferring back to a smaller boat.

It was nighttime when they were brought across a crazily peaceful bay on a small dinghy, angling for a long, wooden dock. The lights of a large resort lit up the ledge on the left side of the sheltered bay. Melene could hear upbeat music and see an outdoor party going on at a large pool that overlooked the ocean. How would they remain incognito if they spent time with that large crowd? Or maybe they were hiding in the crowd. She had no clue how hiding from psychopathic generals worked.

Aiden had a baseball cap and sunglasses on and she had her hair covered and her face partially wrapped in a shawl. She'd seen a gun on his hip and wondered what other weapons he had. On the ships, she'd seen him toying with a knife he seemed to always have in his pocket, but he hadn't worn a pistol since that first night.

A man from the Navy ship handed them up onto the dock, then tossed Aiden's large waterproof backpack up. They hadn't exchanged names with anybody since they left Aiden's SEAL team on that submarine. Melene felt detached and miserable and so, so tired.

The only other emotion she had was gratitude for Aiden and his solid comfort. He'd proven himself patient, kind, and witty as they'd gone through their torturous sea journey. He'd told her stories from his time with the Navy and stories from home to distract her. He was similar to how she remembered him from high school, just more handsome with bigger muscles and a little darker humor. He'd made her laugh even through her seasick misery. Especially when he told stories of his "ugly" twin Thor and the trouble they used to get into. She remembered a few of the pranks but hadn't known who was to blame.

The night air was salty and fresh and she took a few slow, cleansing breaths to settle her stomach. Even though they were off the ship, everything still seemed to rock. Maybe the dock was rocking from the waves created by their small boat.

Shouldering his bag, Aiden thanked the man and took her arm. The man motored away. Melene walked unsteadily up the dock, grateful for Aiden's constant support. Where would she be without him? Lying in a mess of puke in the dark cabin of a military ship somewhere.

No. She glanced at his strong profile in the soft light. She'd be dead without him—or in General Phillip's hands, which would be a fate worse than death.

Aiden was an amazing man and her personal hero. Her Aquaman. If only she could give him one sweet kiss of gratitude. But no. She had to stay strong and not get her heart or his in a bind when they went their separate ways. Also, she needed some strong toothpaste and mouthwash and definitely mint-flavored floss and maybe even some mints or gum to rid her mouth of this taste.

She glanced around at the horseshoe-shaped beach lit with tiki lamps. There were lay-down beach chairs with thatched umbrellas perched above each pair of chairs, a bar, and a small outdoor restaurant. A stack of paddleboards and kayaks were next to the dock. All was quiet and deserted, but she imagined tomorrow afternoon this place would be bustling.

"You all right?" Aiden asked softly as they walked off the dock and through a hard-packed sand trail past the restaurant before they reached some wooden steps. Thankfully, his hand on her elbow steadied her.

"Just feeling a little tipsy," she said.

He chuckled. "You'll fit right in here." He gestured with his chin to their left where the party at the pool was partially visible on the bluff a couple hundred yards away.

"Are we going to stay at this resort?" She doubted General Phillip really had connections in every corner of the world like he seemed to believe, but she'd prefer to stay out of sight until he gave up on pursuing her. If she had a million-dollar price on her head and the general could get her picture and the word out, she might be in danger anywhere in the world.

She was grateful Aiden was with her for however long she needed to hide out, but she wondered how they'd both handle the boredom. They were used to being busy and needed. Children and teenagers competed for her attention all day long. Some volunteers complained the children were draining, but Melene gained energy from their vitality, simple humor, and zest for life. Even in the midst of heartbreaking circumstances, the children usually kept smiling. They taught her more than she taught them most of the time.

"Yes," he said.

They climbed lots and lots of steps.

"But not that section of the resort."

As they reached the top of the steps, he directed her to the right. She wished she knew what direction they were walking and what country or island they were on. She was so drained she didn't even ask.

The path was lit by tiki lamps and made of wooden slats. They walked through thick vegetation. She imagined a bike ride would be a nightmare on these paths, but the sauntering walk was lovely. Her stomach seemed to settle, finally, and her legs that were so used to action and running races with the children were grateful to be moving again after three days on boats. She'd been so sick she'd been unable to walk and unable to move much at all.

"We're in the private villa side. On our honeymoon, you see."

She pulled in a breath and looked at him. Aiden winked and gave her a charming grin. Her body immediately heated in an unfamiliar way.

"Don't worry, my beautiful wife."

She *was* worried ... about him calling her his beautiful wife.

"We've got a two-bedroom, two-bath villa, the room service staff have been generously tipped already and asked to leave all of our food requests outside on the front porch table, and we've requested no maid service for our stay. I know you can hardly wait to be alone with me for ... an undetermined amount of time."

She pasted on a smile as if all was well and pushed away the longing his words had produced. Would she ever have a honeymoon and a handsome husband? Her mom and Grammy Larue bemoaned she never would settle down and go home. Her path was different from her mom's or grandmother's and she rarely dwelt on a husband or any kind of home, but if she could have a husband like Aiden ...

She snuck another glance, and he gave her his easy grin. Of course Aiden was teasing her and maybe putting on the façade in case there was anyone around. He couldn't possibly want to be a on a honeymoon, even a fake one, with someone with dirty, stringy hair, a pale face with blood vessels burst under her eyes from throwing up, who probably reeked of puke and sweat. She couldn't even stand the taste of her own mouth.

She rolled her eyes at herself. What did her looks or smell matter right now? She was running for her life and her virtue from the vile General Phillip. She wasn't after some romance with the attractive and accomplished SEAL from back home. No matter how appealing and incredible he was. They'd get through this time and then he'd go back to active duty and so would she. Her stomach squirmed again, remembering the matter-of-fact words of that high-ranking officer on the submarine asking her to think about her family and what would happen if Aiden didn't show up next time she was in danger, or if she got someone like Aiden and his buddies killed.

She didn't want to think about any of it. She wanted to take a shower, brush her teeth, climb into clean sheets, and sleep until she could sleep no longer. Was that going to happen tonight? At least she had a fighting chance of *that* dream becoming a reality.

The dream of her and Aiden on a honeymoon? She didn't let herself look at him as longing filled her. That dream was *not* reality. It was so far from reality they weren't even in the same neighborhood, zip code, or continent, for heaven's sake. She had to shut that dream down and quick.

They walked on the path for a while, going past a few trails with wooden plaques marking the number of a villa hidden in the trees. It seemed they were going to be a far distance from any neighbors or wandering eyes. That was good.

"There's a high-voltage perimeter fence around the entire property and security guards monitoring the gate and the beaches," Aiden told her. "Not that any of those guards have information about us, but they will provide an extra layer of security and information. Also, Papa hired someone to install security cameras and sensors inside and outside our villa with alerts sent to my phone and his."

"That's good. Papa thinks of everything." She'd noticed the level of respect those high-ranking Navy officers on the ship the first day had given to Admiral Delta. Was Aiden's grandfather still involved in the Navy, or had he called in favors for her? She appreciated him either way.

"Oh, you have no idea."

She hoped they would have toiletries and clothes here at the villa or some way to buy them. She was definitely no spoiled girl. She'd lived in dirt huts and under the stars. She'd be fine without clean clothes; she could scrub these out and they'd dry while she slept. Washing clothes in rivers or lakes was commonplace for her.

She might not survive without a toothbrush, though. Aiden had given her that military toiletry kit and found her clean clothes as often as he could. She'd tried to keep herself clean on the ships, but it had been rough. Sadly, she'd been so out of it that she'd left the kit on the last boat.

"How big is the property?" she asked.

"The specs I was given said four miles long and a half mile wide. There are twelve specialty restaurants, four buffets, seven bars, ten family swimming pools, four adult swimming pools, volleyball, basketball, pickleball, tennis, a movie theater, a bowling alley, a flow rider, a water park, a theater for singing and dancing performances, a fully equipped gym, an incredible spa complete with its own heated pool and hydrotherapy section, snorkeling, scuba diving, their own dolphin experience, kayaks, paddleboards, dancing lessons, more excursions to waterfalls, ziplines, rum factories, shopping, dining, sightseeing tours, and river rafting experiences than you can imagine ... What am I forgetting?"

They walked to what looked to be the end of the trail. She'd noticed at each villa trail there'd been a wider road leading the other direction. They'd tried to hide the road by dense foliage and no lights; presumably the road was for housekeeping and room service vehicles to have access to the villas.

"It sounds like you have done an impressive amount of reconnaissance and this resort has thought of everything."

He led her down the trail of villa #18. "It appears to be a gorgeous, well-maintained, and incredible resort. I read the brochure a few times while you were ... recovering from throwing up."

"Glad you had something to occupy your time."

He smirked at her, not seeming the least put out that he'd had to watch her go through that awfulness. Aiden had been so attentive, patient, and unfazed by her puking disgustedness she'd think he had nursing training, not combat and special ops.

"Thank you again for … taking care of me every which way," she said.

Aiden lifted his eyebrows. "It's in the job description."

"I have some money saved, but I couldn't possibly pay what you're worth. I might be able to repay Papa Delta for at least the cost of staying here," she said, embarrassed. She made okay money because the owner of Health for All insisted full-time workers were paid, and she'd saved most of her money.

"Keep your money," Aiden said easily, as if that was the least of their concerns. He gave her an appealing smirk. "Papa would be offended if you tried to pay him, and there are many benefits to this assignment for me that have nothing to do with money."

Melene's eyes widened. Did he think … what did he expect of her? They were all alone here, and Aiden was a good Christian man so she knew he wouldn't pressure her, but … Her mind was racing.

He stopped walking and so did she. He squeezed her arm softly. "Melene, your brown eyes got very serious and concerned there. I didn't mean … anything untoward. I was just saying it's not a hard job being stuck with a sweetheart like you on a gorgeous island resort."

"Thanks," she managed. She appreciated him in so many ways, and she had no idea how she'd keep her distance emotionally or physically if she was healthy and he was so kind and appealing. She turned to look at their place.

The trees opened up and a quaint front porch complete with rocking chairs decorated the front of their personal villa. It looked a lot more spacious than she'd expected. The exterior had wide, clapboard white siding and bright red shutters framing picture windows.

"It's so charming." Melene clapped her hands together, the lingering nausea finally seeming to disappear in the face of this beautiful private oasis. She and Aiden, pretending to be newly-weds? She risked a glance at him, and he was smiling warmly at her. No, no, no. She could not let her mind keep wandering back to that idea. Far too tempting to forget this was very temporary and he was only here on assignment, no matter if he was much more charming than their cottage.

"Unfortunately for us, we won't be using any of the resort's many fun amenities, but you get the pleasure of being stuck in this little villa with yours truly, your 'charming' Navy SEAL in your 'charming' cottage." He winked and set his bag on the porch. Melene feared he had mind-reading powers.

"I prefer Aquaman," she teased, finally feeling a little more like herself.

"That settles it. I was leaning that direction anyway, but there's the push I needed to grow my hair out and get a few ... dozen more tattoos."

They both laughed.

"Wait ... more?" she asked. "Where are you hiding these tattoos?" That was probably a too-probing question.

His eyes glinted as he lifted the sleeve covering his right bicep. He had a tattoo of what she recognized as the Navy SEAL symbol

43

in black ink: the eagle with a pistol, trident, and anchor in its talons.

She looked it over, her gaze lingering on the striated muscle of his shoulder and upper arm. "I like it," she declared. She wanted to reach out and trail her fingers over it, but she refrained. "You already have the trident. I guess you are Aquaman."

He lifted his eyebrows and grinned. "There you go."

"Do you have ... other tattoos?" She had a feeling she should stop asking.

"A couple." He put a hand to his heart. "I'll show you this one soon." He winked.

Melene's pulse was racing out of control. She probably shouldn't have asked. She really shouldn't want him to whip off his shirt and show her whatever he'd tattooed over his heart.

Oh, boy. She needed some sleep, and she needed distance from her Aquaman.

Chapter Five

Melene turned from staring into Aiden's impossibly blue eyes and looked at the chairs on the front patio. "This entire patio is so welcoming. If I ever have a house someday ..." She broke off. Would she ever have a house? When she'd felt her calling so deeply at eighteen to care for children around the world, she'd been too young and idealistic to stop and think about a future home and family. She missed home and she loved her family, but a family of her own still seemed out of reach.

Aiden didn't say anything, and she wondered if he related to the feeling of not having a home.

Thankfully, he turned and typed in a code on the door rather than delving into it.

The door beeped, and he pressed down the lever and swung it wide, gesturing Melene through first. She stepped inside and gasped, staring around at the most beautiful resort suite she'd ever seen.

Aiden came in after her, set his bag down, and dead bolted the door behind him. He whistled. "Wow. That beats a rack on a sub."

"Beats the tent I usually call home."

He glanced at her. "Please stay right here for a moment."

She nodded and he strode off, checking every nook and cranny and going into what she assumed were the bedrooms.

She took in the details of their villa when he disappeared into a bedroom. Low lighting was on, making everything look even more beautiful and far too romantic for the intimacy of being here alone with the likes of Aiden Delta. When was he going to show her that tattoo and how was she going to resist staring at his chest or reaching out to touch it? Where was tattoo number three? She hoped she could see and touch it as well. She bit at her lip and focused on their surroundings.

The main area was open, with a beautiful kitchen on the right-hand side. It had bright white cabinets, stainless steel appliances, and white and gray swirled granite countertops. There were treats displayed on one countertop, and the four-person table was set with china and crystal with a gorgeous tropical floral arrangement in the center. The rest of the room was spacious and open with a couple leather couches, recliners, and a huge screen television on the wall next to the dining area. The entire back wall was glass. The blinds were open and a sparkling blue infinity pool was lit up with some plush patio furniture and an outdoor dining space next to it.

"I'm told that trail leads down to our own private beach," Aiden said.

"I can't even imagine the views in the daytime." She tried to avoid the images of a private beach. With Aiden shirtless and showing her his other tattoos. Oh boy. Maybe the tattoo over his heart was of some other woman's name. That would definitely help Melene's suddenly too-active imagination.

Lush greenery and flowers were visible around the pool, and deep blue stretched beyond that. Sky or water or both. She couldn't distinguish the separation in the dark.

"I can't wait for daytime." Aiden gave her a grin that made her feel like they were on an adventure, not running for their lives. She couldn't imagine what they'd do holed up for days. Even in this beautiful villa with the pool and beach access, she would get bored, and she could only imagine how restless Aiden would get.

She pushed away all the drama and questions and focused on the adventure part. "Can we go explore the beach quick?"

He laughed. "Sure."

Melene grabbed his hand and tugged him toward the rear patio doors. She suddenly felt more carefree than she had in years. She still needed a shower, toothbrush, and bed, but the idea of exploring a hidden beach through this beautiful jungle made her happy, and made her forget her worries and stress.

Aiden slid open the patio door and they walked past the gorgeous pool area, breathing in the scent of jasmine, plumeria, lime, and eucalyptus trees. The Navy higher-up guy had said they were going to the Caribbean. Melene had worked on various Caribbean islands.

"What island are we even on?" she asked, her energy renewed as they found the trail to the beach off to the left. She released his hand and led the way down the wooden plat staircase.

"Jamaica, mon," he said from behind her.

She laughed. "That fits."

"Somebody is feeling a lot better," Aiden said.

Melene reached the last step and walked through the shadowy trees to a soft sand beach. The ocean was so calm it gently lapped against the sand. She couldn't see much as the moon was covered by clouds, but she inhaled the salt, sand, and wonderful tropical scents.

"Get me on land that doesn't rock and I'm usually happy, low-maintenance, and I often stop projectile vomiting."

Aiden laughed. "You never hit me, at least."

"Small blessings." Leaning down, she slid off her Chacos and plunged her feet into the sand. She closed her eyes and moaned happily. "Ah, I can already feel myself being connected to the earth and my stress melting away."

Aiden said nothing, and she opened her eyes to look at his face. His blue eyes were twinkling at her as if he found her amusing. "I didn't know you were a 'grounding' kind of girl."

"You don't know much at all about me, Aiden Delta."

"I know you're really good at throwing up."

"Ah! Take it back, or I'll ..." She looked around for something to threaten him with. As if she could threaten a man twice her size with muscles prettier than Aquaman's.

He chuckled and folded his arms across his broad chest. He should've looked intimidating, but instead he looked impressive, protective, and awe-inspiring. She glanced away.

"What are you going to threaten me with?" he asked.

"I'll ... push you into the ocean."

He laughed louder. "No, please don't throw me in the ocean. You know I'm terrified of the salty sea."

She shook her head at his silliness, grabbed his arm, and started tugging him toward the water's edge. "Then that is where you're going for making fun of a sickly, frail old woman."

He looked her over, and she wished her eyes hadn't adjusted to the darkness. That look was so full of heat it made her quiver. He planted his feet and she couldn't pull him anywhere. "Sickly, frail, and old?" His smile was a charming smirk that she wanted to kiss right off his face. "Somehow none of those descriptors fit."

She was in such trouble thinking she could withstand Aiden Delta while being alone with him like this, and in a beautiful tropical setting to boot. Why had she suggested they explore the beach? She had to cool the heat singeing the air between them. They'd just gotten here and already she wanted to fling herself against that beautiful chest of his—after he showed her his covered tattoos.

"How about covered in puke, stringy hair, sweaty, in need of a good meal, a toothbrush, a shower, clean clothes, and a little makeup and perfume?" She tilted her head and gave him a challenging look. "How are those descriptors?"

His smirk turned to a full-on grin. "Yep, those fit pretty well."

Though she'd given him the descriptors, she still gasped in outrage, but then she couldn't help but laugh. She'd forgotten how fun it was to tease with a man, especially a man as irresistible as Aiden.

"Let me help you change those descriptors." His voice was full of teasing, but also a delicious promise. How was he going to help her?

Aiden closed the distance between them and swooped her off her feet before she could protest or dodge away. He pulled her in tight to that well-muscled chest of his and her breath left her lungs in a rush. Her heart raced uncontrollably, and she prayed she didn't stink. He smelled like he'd showered recently and brushed his teeth.

Dang him. He had. When she was trying to get herself off the bed on the last ship as they told them they were putting down anchor to disembark. He'd gone and showered quick.

"You're not supposed to smell good," she hurled at him.

He grinned and his cheek crinkled irresistibly. His blue eyes were so bright and alluring. She hadn't been around many handsome, blue-eyed men the past few years. Come to think of it, she hadn't been around many men, period. Mostly women and children were who she worked with and helped. The men were either off working to secure the necessities of life, in the military, or sadly had been killed and left their families alone in the aftermath of some of the war-torn areas she'd served in.

"You don't smell good," he teased her.

Melene gasped again and tried to pull away from him.

He held her tighter, laughing at his own rude comment as he plunged them through the sand and into the water. "Don't worry, I'll help you clean up."

Melene had to wrap her arms around his neck to stabilize herself. She tried not to breathe on him and have him smell her rotten breath. How she longed for a toothbrush. Hopefully the resort provided basic toiletries.

All of those worries were pushed aside as Aiden plunged them into the ocean until he was chest deep. "Hold your breath," he cautioned.

She took a breath and he ducked under, tugging her with him. The warm water embraced her, but Aiden's arms around her was a better embrace than the ocean or anything she'd experienced.

They surfaced and water glistened off his handsome face and dripped from his short hair. "Better?" he asked.

She laughed and pushed away from him, though it was the last thing she wanted to do. She swam deeper into the ocean and he followed her with easy strokes. He was obviously a natural in the water.

"You love the water?" she asked.

"It's my home. My favorite place on earth."

She smiled, wishing she was his home and his favorite place on earth, which was a little weird to even think. She wasn't a place and had no home to offer anyone. She was a simple woman who had never and might never settle down.

Rolling over, she floated on her back and looked up at the deep-blue sky. She relaxed and felt more comfortable and at peace than she had since she'd run from General Phillip. No, that wasn't accurate. This was more peaceful than she'd felt in years.

Aiden's hand wrapped around hers and she startled before settling back into the water. She turned her head slightly so she could see him. His profile was striking. To see his well-built chest floating so close by, and have his hand wrapped around hers, was comforting and stimulating.

Her ears started feeling the pressure of floating for too long, and she righted herself. Aiden released her hand and they treaded water next to each other. "Thanks," she said.

"Of course. I'm always up for float therapy."

She smiled. The water had revitalized her as it always did, and being close to Aiden was like a caffeine shot, but the exhaustion of not sleeping well, being so ill, hardly eating, and danger chasing them was overwhelming her. She yawned.

"Let's go find you a shower, clean clothes, a bed, and maybe that toothbrush."

"Thank you." She splashed water at him. "But the toothbrush comment was pushing it." Though she agreed, she hated the thought of him thinking her breath was disgusting.

He laughed. "You were the one who said you needed one."

"You've been around a bunch of men for too long, Aiden my friend. Here's a tip—never tell a woman she stinks."

He tilted his chin up and smiled. "Thanks. I'll try to remember that."

She looked over his broad shoulders with his T-shirt clinging to his shoulders and chest and then she let her eyes feast on his handsome, sculpted face. Even in the dim light, his blue eyes got to her. "You probably don't need any help where women are concerned."

He shrugged. "Historically, no."

That made jealousy dart through her gut. "What about currently?"

"I seem to be flubbing this one up."

He grinned and she laughed, but then they both went serious far too quickly. Melene thought he was irresistible, but she had to resist him. She could only imagine how quickly women succumbed to his charms. This time with her Aquaman would be here and gone soon. She didn't need her heart tangled up and broken with Aiden as they went their separate ways, back to the lives they both felt called to. He'd told her in the stories he'd used to entertain her on the ship how the SEALs was his calling and purpose in life. She felt the same about her own work.

She didn't want to hurt him, either. He was a fabulous guy.

"Ready for bed?" he asked in a husky voice that sent a tremor through her.

"Ready to sleep in my own bed," she clarified.

"Of course." His teasing tone was back. "What do you think my mama taught me?"

She laughed but didn't comment. His mom was amazing and the Deltas were all strong Christians. She could imagine his "mama" taught him a lot of important lessons.

They swam toward the shore and sloshed up onto the sand, water dripping from their clothes and hair. He still had socks and shoes on, and she noticed he'd forgotten to take off the pistol strapped to his waist. What about his phone?

Reaching down for her Chacos, she straightened and pointed. "You got your gun wet."

He smiled. "The privilege of being a Navy SEAL. My equipment is waterproof and can fire anywhere on the planet."

"I forget how special you are."

"Don't do that."

"Do what?" she asked sassily. "Tease you, or forget how special you are?"

"You can tease me all you want. *Never* forget how special I am." His voice deepened. "Or at least should be to you."

His grin was so appealing she had to force out a laugh, embarrassed when it was husky and unsteady. He was special. He was amazing. She had to somehow resist his appeal. She wanted to ask him if he ever planned to settle down and get married, but that would send all the wrong signals, as if she yearned to be the one he'd marry. He was only teasing and making things fun, and she needed to remember that.

She turned away and headed up the stairs. He followed without saying anything.

They reached the back patio and the pool, still dripping. "I don't want to drip water through that beautiful house," she said.

He looked around and then walked to a shelf by the pool, bending down and pulling two large towels off the lower shelf. She followed him and took one towel from his outstretched hand.

"Perfect. Thank you." She set her shoes down, squeezed some water from her hair with the towel, then wrapped it around her torso and legs.

They were quiet as they made their way back into the house. Aiden locked the patio door behind them and then set an alarm. "Wait just a moment," he cautioned her.

She didn't say anything but watched as he walked into each of the bedrooms and then out and even checked the pantry. "Everything's secure," he said. "I'd get an alert from the sensors or cameras, but I like to make sure."

"Thank you."

He walked to the fridge, retrieved two water bottles, and brought one to her. Their fingers brushed and set off a warmth inside her.

Aiden smiled at her. She uncapped the water bottle and took a long, satisfying, restorative drink to cover her reaction to him. She felt so safe, warm, and taken care of with him around. If only she could bring him with her to her next assignment. She doubted very much she'd get back to Banida or Poland. She wondered where the owner of Health for All, Avalyn Shaman-Hawk, would assign her next. It needed to be somewhere far from General Phillip's reign of terror, like Fiji or Tahiti. There was no shortage of charitable missions with so many people not being born into the privilege and opportunity she had, then to make it worse, evil people created more havoc and poverty through war and selfishness. She felt a pang as she looked around at this beautiful and luxurious retreat. It would be hard to relax knowing so many were suffering.

What about Thomas's family and all those people at the refugee camp? Had Phillip gone after them? She feared he would, but nobody would confirm that to her. Probably because it was true. It made her sick. Sadly, there was nothing she could do besides pray.

Hopefully, twelve hours in a comfortable and clean bed would help restore her normally positive attitude, and help her have the self-control to not beg Aiden to take off his shirt and show off his tattoos and then pull her against that nice chest of his again. It had simply been too long since she'd dated or flirted with a man. It wasn't that Aiden was special to her.

But maybe it was.

"Which room is mine?"

He pointed at the bedroom closest to them. "Your clothes and girly stuff are in the master."

"Clothes and girly stuff?" She suddenly felt lighter. She wouldn't have to subsist in these clothes and with no toiletries until they were given clearance to leave here?

"Yes, ma'am." He grinned and pushed at his wet hair, making his muscles all too evident in that wet T-shirt.

Melene let out a happy cheer, which made him chuckle. She held on to the towel as she rushed for the bedroom door. It was a gorgeous, airy bedroom with an enormous bed covered in a fluffy white comforter, a divan sofa by the huge windows, and white dressers against the other walls. Large windows perpendicular to the bed probably gave a great view of the ocean and greenery in the daytime.

She ran into the attached bath to her left. It had a nice granite shower enclosure, a corner soaking tub, a toilet in its own small room, and a large granite double-sink vanity. There were a multitude of hair products, lotions and perfumes, makeup, and most importantly toothbrush, toothpaste, floss, and mouthwash on the counter. There was also a small walk-in closet with sundresses, swimsuit coverups, and fancy dresses hanging up. On the shelves were stacked shorts, T-shirts, bras, underwear, swimsuits, and socks. There were even some strappy sandals, flip-flops, and running shoes. Would she be able to go on a run through this huge property? Who had been so thorough and generous with her needs?

Melene was used to being the one who showed up with necessities to help people eke out a life barely above survival levels. She always brought her personal backpack with toiletries, her phone, scriptures, her running shoes, and what clothes she could fit. Health for All provided anything else she needed on location, but this was above and beyond. Someone had personally anticipated her every need and made sure that even though she was in survival mode of her own, she would have things to make her beyond comfortable. She found herself strangely emotional and very grateful. Having all of this felt like something her family would do for her, felt like home and someone caring for her in a way she hadn't felt since she was a small child. Scratch that. Aiden had cared for her like this on all those ships and submarines.

She heard Aiden walk in behind her. "Do you have everything you need?"

The contents of the closet were blurry, and she couldn't blink them clear. She dropped the water bottle, spun around, and threw her arms around his neck. "Bless whoever was so thoughtful!"

The towel dropped from around her and she was pressed tightly against him as he returned the hug. "I, um, thought that you would ..."

"You did this?" She should've guessed. Ah, Aiden. How could he keep impressing her more every moment?

"Well, I requested clothes, shoes, and girly stuff." He smiled down at her as if embarrassed that she knew it was him. "I'm sure my mom, Esther, or one of the Delta women is to blame for getting the details right."

"I love your family," she told him, wishing she could better express her gratitude, but anything else would compromise her in the worn out state she was in.

"They all love you."

He still held her close, and she felt as if maybe he was saying he loved her, too. How else would something so special and personal happen? No. His thoughtfulness was simply Aiden being a with-it Delta and his comment was a platonic, 'yes my family is great, we all love you like a member of the community from home' kind of comment. Right?

Sometimes she craved home and often she missed her family. With Aiden holding her close, and all these unnecessary but thoughtful comforts surrounding her, she felt a sense of home even thousands of miles from their Colorado valley.

Aiden's gaze dipped to her lips and the room was suddenly very hot. He was going to kiss her. Was he really? Time stalled and desire filled her. One kiss wouldn't be out of line. She could call it a kiss of gratitude.

As his eyes lifted to hers, she saw a vulnerability and need she never thought this tough SEAL would reveal. She let out a longing sigh.

He blinked and suddenly something shifted. He eased away from her, and she should've felt awkward, but the longing for him was too strong to feel anything but the desire to throw herself against him and kiss him if he wasn't going to initiate.

Oh, my. She needed some distance and now, or she *would* initiate that kiss and make things awkward for the rest of their stay. Or, if a kiss with Aiden was anywhere close to as incredible as it felt being held close to him, she'd lose her heart, show him how lacking she'd been in romance the past few years, kiss until they were ready to leave, and get her own heart broken. He obviously dated a lot of women and moved on easily. He also obviously wasn't the type to settle down, and neither was she. She wasn't special to him and if she remembered right, Aiden was the type who flirted and teased with every girl.

"Thank you." She pulled back. "I'll see you in the morning."

He nodded, turned, and hurried from the room, shutting the door softly behind him.

Melene stood there for a minute, reeling with the loss of what might have been. Then she headed for the shower. She'd learned not to let herself get overly emotional. Even though she adored the families she helped, especially the children, crying or moaning about how much they lacked or how hard their lives were would only burn her out and make her unable to keep serving. It was the same with Aiden. Stewing about kissing and holding him would only make her long for what she could never have, and that was a waste of time and emotional resources.

A shower was a fabulous idea. Being clean and then sleeping a long time would help her get her head on straight. Lots of prayer would be needed too.

She hoped rooting out this desire for Aiden was even possible at this point. There had been many times over the past ten years she'd let her heart get too entangled in the people she served, and it had about destroyed her. She hoped she wasn't in too deep with her handsome Navy SEAL rescuer already. It had only been a few days since he'd appeared like an angelic Aquaman. It seemed the desire, appreciation, and enjoyment of Aiden's personality, kindness, and entire being were already deeply embedded in her heart.

Please, someone in heaven help me be strong so I can continue to ease burdens.

It was a prayer she prayed often, and she felt it was answered often. Right now, this prayer took a different direction. She hoped *she* was strong enough to let heaven help. When Aiden was close, she had little desire for her own strength and far too much desire for his to surround her. Yikes. That was something she couldn't let herself think about, or she might rush into his bedroom and beg him to hug her again.

Chapter Six

Aiden had awoken periodically throughout the night, checking the sensors and cameras and doing a perimeter and house sweep, except for Melene's room, only listening to make sure her breathing was even.

His phone was beeping an alert.

He grabbed it off the nightstand, shooting up in bed. The phone said eight-thirteen local time, and the sun was trying to peek through the window shutters. He never slept that late, but he instinctively felt safe in this tropical and remote location. Or maybe it was Melene who made him feel grounded and safe and like he was home.

He pushed that away and clicked on the alert. He saw a woman dressed in a white uniform carrying a large tray to their front door. She set the tray on the porch table, rapped softly on the door, and then turned and strode off.

He scrambled out of bed, threw a T-shirt on, grabbed his gun and knife, and hurried out of his bedroom and into the entryway. Checking each of the cameras on his phone, he didn't see any other movement around the property. The only red flag was he hadn't thought to put a room service order in last night. Too tired and too twisted up thinking of Melene until he'd fallen into an exhausted slumber.

He texted Papa quickly.

Room service?

I ordered it for you. Figured you'd both be starving.

Thank you.

He disabled the alarms, retrieved the food, shut and locked the door, and armed it again. The food smelled delicious, but he needed to exercise first, and he could wait for Melene to wake up to eat.

He'd had brief workouts on the ships when Melene had fallen into an exhausted slumber from her seasickness, but mostly he'd had far too much inactivity the past few days. His body felt achy and uncomfortable from the lack of movement, and his mind definitely needed the boost only a good workout could provide.

He carried the tray in and set it on the kitchen counter, slipping the fruit, yogurt, juices and milk in the fridge and then lifting the plates of bacon, French toast, and omelets into the oven and hitting the keep warm button.

He looked through his phone for any emails or text updates on their situation. Papa had sent a report early this morning and had said room service had been ordered. He smiled. Should've read through his texts before shooting the question off earlier. General Phillip seemed busy overseeing troop training and movement and probably strategizing with King Frederick how to overthrow Poland and Germany at the same time. They were both psychos who would be smacked down quick when they tried to mess with countries with strong militaries and strong allies.

Aiden texted Papa everything was very beautiful, luxurious, and quiet here, and then pocketed his phone and went to check on Melene.

Melene's door was slightly ajar. He crept close and leaned his head to the side, hoping to hear all was well with her without actually intruding on her privacy. Teasing her came very naturally to him. He had to keep up some boundaries and insulate his heart from the exotic and charitable beauty. It had been torture to step back rather than kiss her last night. All too soon, this assignment would be done, and he wanted to make sure they both walked away with positive feelings and no heart issues.

He heard soft, even breathing. Good. She was still sleeping soundly as she had throughout the night. She needed some rest and recuperation after all the stress of escaping from and having a bounty put on her head by General Phillip, and how miserable she'd been on the different ships, subs, and boats. Poor thing. She'd been so sweet, innocent, and fragilely beautiful as he'd taken care of her while she was sick. He cared deeply for Melene. As his assignment and a friend from home. That's how he had to compartmentalize it.

He needed some time to work out and get himself ready to be fun and teasing but keep his distance. With Melene being so ... Melene, that was going to be extremely rough.

There wasn't a ton of space and no home gym equipment. He wished he dared take Melene to the gym on the property, but Phillip was well-connected and wealthy. From what Papa's contacts had reported, his million-dollar offer and photos of Melene were being circulated around the globe. A few years ago, there were many places they could've hidden and the locals would've never known there was a bounty on his assignment's head. Now it seemed internet access was as common as rice consumption. He'd seen mothers in the Philippines holding their babies while living on top of a cardboard box, gripping a cell phone as tightly as they did their own children. It was insane, and it made it harder to hide in plain sight.

He set up a circuit of pushups, pullups, tricep dips, planks, burpees, lunges, jump squats, and jumping jacks. After an hour, he was sweating profusely in the tropical air, even in the shade of the thick trees surrounding the pool, and he still had his shirt on. It was silly, but he'd loved teasing with Melene last night about the tattoo over his heart. He wanted to have some significant reveal of both of his covered tattoos, not just have her see them and that was that.

His buddies would chortle if they knew he was planning tattoo reveals to a beautiful woman. Aiden was hit on by many women wherever they went, as were most of his friends and team-mates. The tough, unreachable special ops men seemed to be ultra-appealing to a lot of women.

Sometimes he and his buddies had time to take a pretty girl out to dinner, but usually not. A few of their team had developed long-term relationships with women near their home base in Little Rock, Virginia. Aiden had never found a woman he wanted to go on more than a few dates with and he also hated the idea of leaving some lady pining for him and waiting on his return, or worse, broken emotionally if he never returned. It wasn't fair to her, and it could mess with his ability to stay detached and focused on each mission.

Jace's wife had been broken emotionally, and he hadn't even died. He'd gone home one day to find his father-in-law waiting to inform him they'd admitted Charisse to a hospital that specialized in body image issues. She had extreme anorexia and the root of her disorder was trying to be perfect physically so her husband would someday choose her over his missions. Charisse sent him divorce papers the day she was released from the hospital. Aiden had been there as Jace signed the papers. He told him he loved Charisse and he wanted her happy and healthy. He'd never chosen her over his missions and that was all she'd wanted. Aiden didn't want to ever have to make that heart-wrenching choice and still saw the pain in his friend's eyes far too often.

A couple of the other guys had also gone through divorces, coming home to find their wife cheating. Only one of their team-mates, Riley, was married. From what the rest of them observed, it was rough on him and on his wife of only two years to be apart so often. Aiden tried not to join in the speculation of if the couple would last. The special ops divorce rate was last reported to him at eighty percent. Not the most encouraging number.

He forced all worries of relationships, marriage, and divorce from his mind. Where had that even come from? Maybe it was his family getting bitten by the love bug. His hilarious twin brother Thor was getting married in ... was it three days or four? He sadly knew he wouldn't make it, so he hadn't firmed the date in his mind and let himself bemoan missing the most important date of one of the most important people in his life. No matter how much time they spent apart, he and Thor were inseparably connected.

His strong but silent brother Greer and rock-steady sweetheart of a sister Esther had recently found the love of their lives. His parents, aunt and uncle and grandparents all had wonderful marriages, or had as Granny had passed a long while ago.

Marriage was great. For people who could settle down. Aiden definitely wasn't in that population sector. He imagined he'd be a SEAL until Papa requested him to come home permanently to protect the Delta secret, the Navy forced him out because of injury, or he got killed. Being alone hadn't bothered him much. Until the past few days of being around Melene. Even as sick as she'd been, he'd felt drawn to her, wanted to take care of and protect her, and had been impressed with how little she'd complained and how sweet and grateful she'd been.

Hurrying back into the house, he downed a water bottle and took a shower. He dressed in a T-shirt and hybrid shorts that would be comfortable in the water or out, strapping back on his Glock 19 and pocketing his knife and phone. Hopefully Melene was open to spending a lot of time in the water. He didn't know what else they'd do here holed up in their private oasis. He'd have to stay vigilant watching the cameras, sensors, and for any signs of danger or someone snooping around, but he thought it would be all right if they went back down to that private beach. With his high-tech phone and waterproof gun, they could swim and mess around in the water to get some energy out.

Not *mess around*, mess around.

He wandered back into the bathroom to brush his short hair and put on some deodorant. By mess around, he was thinking he could launch her into the air or she could try to dunk him, not kissing for long periods of time in only swimsuits.

65

Wow. Was the air conditioning even working in this place?

He checked the app on his phone that Papa had sent. It was set at seventy. That was a reasonable temperature. Maybe even cool for a house. Dang.

He paced his bedroom, needing to be calm and ready to face the day with Melene before he went into the main area. He had to make a solid plan of what else he and Melene could do that did not involve kissing or hugging or ... He'd teased her about being on their honeymoon. If they were really on their honeymoon, he could imagine this would be paradise, but he ... could not let his mind go to marriage or honeymoons.

He turned the air down to sixty-eight. Hopefully that wouldn't be too cold for Melene.

So what would they do? Play cards? Watch movies? Swap stories? Swap saliva? Good crap. She wasn't even awake and already his mind was wandering.

He knew what downtime was, and sometimes he even experienced it, but his team usually tried to maximize even wait time with training, exercise, research, and strategizing. Jace was an incredible leader and a crazy hard worker.

Aiden walked back out into the main area ... and stopped in his tracks. His jaw slackened and his body was instantly warm.

Melene was in the swimming pool. There weren't inside sensors and alerts to movement as that would be annoying and like crying wolf, but he should've checked the cameras to prepare himself for this. She was distracting him, which was just another reason he shouldn't get involved.

Her back was to him. She was jumping around, punching her arms up and down, then running in place, then flinging her body side to side. He assumed it was some sort of … jazzercise in a swimming pool, with no music. It was adorable and far too appealing.

He'd seen many women in swimming suits. He hadn't seen Melene in one since one of her friends had organized swim lessons in his family's lake. She'd looked good then but hadn't developed fully into a woman. The suit she had on now was a pale pink one piece that showed off her smooth, dark skin and her incredible shape to perfection.

She turned in a circle in her jumping, punching, and dancing state and stopped with her arms in the air, staring at him. Slowly lowering her arms, she backed into the side of the infinity pool.

"No, don't stop," he begged.

The patio door was shut, so she couldn't hear him. He hurried to the glass door, slid it open, and strode out. "Please don't stop," he said. "That was adorable."

Melene shook her head. "I can't believe you saw that. I've been puking all over the place for days, I was stinky and ugly last night, and now you catch me doing water aerobics. How awkward am I?"

"Not awkward at all, though some music might make it more fun." He wanted her to keep dancing in the water, in her swimsuit. It was fun, lighthearted, would distract both of them, give her exercise, and make his heart race out of control. He wished he could tell her she could never be ugly and that he'd been around sweaty men for far too long, he hadn't even noticed if she smelled bad. He'd simply been teasing her last night.

He pulled his phone out and opened the Spotify app. "Any requests?"

She swirled the water between her fingers. A shaft of sun penetrated the trees surrounding the pool area and sparkled off her dark hair and trim shoulders. The one-piece suit was modest, but it dipped in the front and dipped even deeper in the back. Not that he was staring. He was definitely staring. How could Melene be so innocent yet sensual at the same time?

"I'm not going to keep dancing while you watch me," she protested.

"I'll do it with you. You can be the teacher and I'll willingly do any dance move you ask me to do." He hoped that didn't come across as too flirtatious. Even if he really would.

"The Navy SEAL has moves?"

He chuckled. He wasn't some incredible dancer, but his fun-loving cousin Maddie had taught him how to stay on beat. "Oh, you have no idea," he told her.

Her dark eyes glinted. A challenge or an invitation, he couldn't be sure.

He found a Spotify clean dance station and pushed play. Pocketing his phone, he didn't even think about taking off his gun, even though the pool was miniscule.

He jumped into the pool, tucking his knees into his chest to create a bigger splash. He heard Melene cry out. He hit the concrete bottom and pushed back up, flinging out of the water and imitating her cheerleader looking jumps with his arms splayed.

"Let's jazzercise," he called out, trying to move to the beat with his arms up in the air and his abdomen and hips swiveling. The water slowed down his movements, so he had to go faster.

He should've taken his T-shirt off, but there was still the matter of the tattoo reveal being perfect. It shouldn't even be something he was thinking about as he knew neither he nor

Melene could have a long-term relationship, but it was hard not to plot and strategize intimate moments with a woman as irresistible as Melene so close.

Melene wiped water from her face that he'd put there from his cannonball and folded her trim arms over her chest. "It's not jazzercise," she said primly. "It's water conditioning."

He chuckled. "Condition me then, beautiful lady."

She shook her head and then she rewarded him with a light, tinkling laugh. It was great to hear her laugh, especially after how terrified she'd been when they were escaping the general and then her being so sick. It was still surreal he'd come upon Melene at the right moment to rescue her and now he was protecting her. So far it was the best protection detail he'd ever been part of.

She started dancing to the beat, and he imitated every silly and sexy move she made. They laughed and splashed each other and he actually got his heart rate up, but that might have more to do with how cute and beautiful Melene was at the same time. Cute because she was so fun and could let go and be silly, and beautiful because her gorgeous face and her body in that suit were far too alluring to him.

They'd been going for a while when one of the songs ended and she put up her hands as if in surrender. "All right, you win. You've out-jazzercised me and I am starving."

"Ah shoot, I bet you are." He pointed at her, frustrated at himself for not thinking of that and insisting she eat first. Distracting was too tame a term for Melene's power over him. Absorbing, all-encompassing, enthralling ... he wasn't a literature expert, but those seemed more fitting. He was in trouble. "You wait out here and I'll go warm up and bring all the food out."

She smiled. "I'm not faint from hunger, Aiden. I can help."

"Melene." He gave her a stern look. "You haven't eaten a decent meal in days, you've thrown up any food I managed to coerce down you, and you've just worked up a serious appetite with all this intense water conditioning. I will get the food."

She gave him a sassy look and tried to push past him to the stairs. Aiden grabbed her around the waist and hauled her back against his chest. He was suddenly out of breath and his pulse skyrocketed higher than it had been during his burpees this morning. He found his hands sliding naturally around her waist and her trim body melted back against his.

Instead of fighting or teasing with him, she snuggled against him. Aiden had no idea what to do now, or what to make of her reaction. She was either faint from lack of nourishment or being close to him affected her as much as it did him.

His brain was screaming at him to unhand the beautiful woman. Besides the distraction issue, he wasn't in any kind of position to offer a long-term commitment, and Melene was not the type of woman any man should trifle with.

He tried to remember to tease. "You think you can mess with a Navy SEAL?" he asked, his voice far too husky and telling.

She looked over her shoulder at him. Aiden's breath caught and something lodged in his chest, making it impossible to inhale properly. He needed a regulator and a full oxygen tank. No ... he needed to kiss her exquisite mouth for a very, very long time. Kissing Melene would give him everything he needed.

"I think I have complete power over this Navy SEAL," she said softly.

Aiden's eyes widened. Was he that transparent?

Tease out of this, keep it light, keep it shallow, his rational mind begged, but his body was rebelling.

He chuckled, and it sounded unsteady even to him. He had to move and quick. He had to think as if an enemy had him in his sights and was going to fire and incapacitate him. Melene was the farthest thing from an enemy, but he was in her power and he couldn't allow that. He was on a mission. Her safety was what mattered, not the out-of-control beating of his heart and the way he was reacting to her soft but firm body so close.

React. Move. Do something, you infatuated wimp, his brain pleaded.

Aiden had been trained by his dad, his Papa, his Mama, and the best, and sometimes harshest, instructors the United States Navy had to offer. He was strong mentally, physically, and spiritually. He could instinctively keep Melene and himself safe from whatever this crazy and illogical reaction to holding her was. He'd made it through BUD/S training without ringing the bell. Somehow, he'd survive this.

He moved his hands to her hips and easily lifted her out of the pool and onto the side. She gasped in surprise, bending her legs. He released her and hurried up the steps past her as she straightened. "I'll get the food. You sit and relax," he instructed. It came out too harsh and demanding, but he had to be decisive and get some distance from her, or more accurately, from his reaction to her.

She luckily didn't say anything as he strode to the back door, dripping wet. He stripped off his shirt and dropped it by the back door and grabbed a towel from the rack, wrapping it around his waist and then pushing the patio door open and rushing inside.

He didn't let himself look at Melene or think about how incredible she looked and felt to him. He'd try to convince himself he simply hadn't held a woman close for a while, but he was lying to himself. Melene was special. She was especially special to him. Which sounded cheesy and not like him at all.

He hurried to grab the food out of the oven. It was warm but not hot. He took the first plate and shoved it in the microwave, hitting the minute button.

Looking down, he realized his chest tattoo was revealed. Dang it. He wanted to show Melene in a special moment.

He hung his head and said a brief prayer for strength and to keep his head on straight so he could protect Melene. Neither of them needed or could afford a romantic entanglement.

Please help, he begged heaven above.

The good Lord had kept him safe on so many missions he could only express gratitude each time. He knew how diligently his family, especially his sweet mom, always prayed for him at home. Right now, he felt like he was in a battlefield and he could only pray for help, strength, and guidance.

He ran his hand through his hair as he turned from the microwave and made the mistake of looking out the back wall of glass.

Melene stood there in her swimsuit. Her body was enticing to him, but it was the longing look in her dark eyes that he had no clue how to resist.

Oh, please help, he begged heaven above for what had to be the dozenth time.

What if the help from heaven was bringing Melene into his

life? What if it was time to give up saving the world and focus on loving and saving this incredible woman?

The microwave beeped behind him, preventing him from having to muddle out a question that insane. Melene was his mission for the next few days, not for life. He had to stay strong.

Aiden had always pushed himself hard and been proud of his mental, physical, spiritual, and emotional strength. Who knew a few days with an exotic, smart, and charitable beauty could mess with him on every level?

Chapter Seven

Melene was so confused and stirred up by Aiden. She found it very interesting as he brought the breakfast back out that he'd put on a dry T-shirt and he seemed to have put a mask over his emotions. He was fun and teasing and bright and happy. She knew those were all facets of Aiden's personality, but he was hiding something right now. Was he as unsettled as she was by the strong emotions and connection that coursed between them? Or was she only hoping he had the same feelings surging through him?

She'd convinced herself last night to keep her distance and be strong. Less than an hour of silly water aerobics with her fun, tough Navy SEAL protector and then him putting his arms around her and pulling her back against his strong body had made everything disappear but him. Her only desire at that moment had been to hold him, be close to him, talk for hours, and kiss for even longer.

Her charitable missions seemed far away. At the moment, it

was hard to concentrate on anything but Aiden. She wanted to tease him about covering up the tattoo on his chest again, but found she couldn't. She hadn't been able to see it clearly through the window earlier, but was suddenly terrified it was some other woman's name. Why else would he not just show her?

She was famished, so she ate the delicious food quickly and ate far too much. Leaning back on the soft patio chair with the tropical sun quickly drying her swimsuit and hair, she said, "Whew. We'd better do more jazzercise. I ate way too much."

Aiden's incredible blue eyes swept over her and the tropical sun couldn't be all to blame for how hot she suddenly was. "I don't think you need to worry about eating too much."

She straightened and gave him a challenging glare. "What is that supposed to mean?"

He smiled. "It was supposed to be a compliment. You look incredible, but you are very thin. You could gain twenty pounds and still be tiny."

She bristled. "Listen, Mr. Buff Aquaman."

He grinned at that.

"I work my tail off every day and it's hard to keep weight on with the heat and the workload, but I do not starve myself." This was a very touchy subject with her mom and Gramma Larue. "I still have womanly curves."

Aiden's eyes widened. "Oh believe me, Melene, I'm very aware that you have womanly curves."

More heat filled her, and she leaned back. She was aware this swimming suit showed off her curves to advantage and it made her happy that he'd noticed. "Well, good. Thank you."

He smirked at her. "My cousin Alivia used to say you were so sweet you'd melt in a rainstorm. Guess you got a little sassy over the years."

Her mouth dropped open again. "These are like the most backwards compliments I have ever received."

He laughed. "I'm sorry. I'm not trying to twist compliments and Alivia meant it in the most complimentary way possible. You have always been kind and charitable." His gaze swept over her again. "But I'm coming to see you have some spice in you, too." His voice got husky. "I like it."

Melene blinked at him. She wanted to ease around this table, plop herself onto his lap, run her fingers through his short hair, and kiss him until lunchtime.

"We'd better clean up breakfast," he said brightly, jumping to his feet and stacking plates onto the tray.

Melene stood as well. Instead of helping, she stared at him. "What are you scared of?"

Aiden froze with a plate in one hand and a cup in the other. He stared down at her and shook his head. "Excuse me?"

She should be the one scared of opening this can of worms, but Aiden was so irresistible. She wanted to be closer to him. She wanted to develop something with him. It was dumb of her, and she had no clue how a relationship could ever work for her with her lifestyle and especially a relationship with someone like Aiden who was as committed and felt "called" to his busy and demanding life and career just like she was.

She eased closer to him. Aiden released the plate and cup with a clatter and backed away from her. She'd said earlier that he was in her power and, wow, did she feel that now. She backed this tough man right up against the glass wall and she pressed her palms flat against his incredible chest.

"What are you afraid of?" she asked softly.

Aiden stared down at her. His blue eyes were soft and vulnerable. She didn't know if he was going to tease her, tell her the truth, run away, or take her in his arms and give her the kiss she was craving.

"Melene," he said just as softly. "You are an amazing woman."

Her breath caught and she bit at her lip, thrilled that the kiss was coming.

His gaze traveled over her face, but instead of pulling her close, he took her hands from his chest and held them in his. "Sadly, we both know this situation is only temporary and with our individual callings in life being all-encompassing ... you and I could never work." He said the words kindly, but they pierced her clear through.

"Ouch," she managed.

"I'm sorry," was all he offered. He wasn't going to take the words back, and he meant them.

Melene felt a dart of pain go through her like an arrow, swift and aimed at her heart. He was right. She was being silly and short-sighted. They could never work, and he was only here to protect her. He was being smart, and she needed to follow his lead. These very logical thoughts didn't stop the hurt, and she felt the sting of emotion like last night in her closet. Only this emotion wasn't gratitude. It was as if she was a teenager being ditched by the most impressive and appealing guy at the school, before they even went on a date.

She stepped back, schooled her features, and pulled her hands free. He watched her as if she would crumble in front of him.

"You're right, and I'm the one who is sorry." She forced a smile and focused on her gratitude for him. "You're amazing too, Aiden, and I really appreciate you rescuing me, taking care of me on all those miserable ships, and being here to protect me and keep things fun now. I'll keep my temporary desires in check and not make this any harder than it has to be for either of us."

He nodded. His blue gaze showed he didn't like this any more than she did.

"I wish it could be different for us," he admitted.

"Me too." She couldn't keep the longing from her voice.

But it couldn't be different. Even if one of them backed out of their callings in life, what would that solve? She couldn't follow him around like a SEAL's puppy. No, that wasn't right. She honored and respected military wives and husbands, thought they were as strong and brave as their spouses, but she knew it wasn't her path.

She guessed he could follow her around and help her with her missions, but was that what he wanted, what he was trained for and excelled at? No. Not even close. He was so impressive, and the world needed men like him.

She drew in a breath and turned away, walking back to the table. They stacked dishes and carried everything to the front door. Aiden set it outside for room service to pick it up. She felt guilty for the food that was wasted and for not washing the dishes first, but Aiden reassured her that was what they were supposed to do.

As they finished, Aiden closed and locked the front door. He set that alarm and turned to her. He folded his arms across his chest and she was awed by the strength there. Strength that would protect her, not hold and comfort her. That was how it had to be. She had to push away the memory of how tender and patient he'd been when she was sick, how fun and appealing he was now, and how his every touch or look seemed to light a fire inside her. It didn't matter and it couldn't go anywhere. No matter how that stunk, she couldn't change it.

Now how to burn through the time until they could safely return to their own lives? Hopefully it was only a day or two or she might go insane trapped with this incredible and beautiful man who was out of reach. They'd both admitted nothing could happen between them, but it stung deeply that he'd said it first. That he could be so rational and in control, not just fling the future worries in the ocean and kiss their time away. Maybe that just meant he wasn't as drawn to her as she was to him.

"So ..." He gave her a grin that made her knees feel weak. "What do you want to do for fun today?"

She shrugged, frustrated at herself for being so susceptible to his every grin and look. But dang those blue eyes of his ... "Do we have many options? We're kind of stuck here, right?"

He nodded. "True. We can go swim in the ocean, though. I can stay armed and monitor my phone in the water. I was thinking I could have room service drop off snorkeling masks and maybe even some scuba gear. Have you ever done an open water dive?"

"No. I've never done any kind of dive, I've hardly even snorkeled." A lot of her missions were in warm places and some by the ocean, but she didn't have a lot of free time or equipment. She did love to swim in the ocean and did that as often as she could.

His grin was irresistible. "Well then, we definitely need to remedy that. They'd probably bring us paddle boards and kayaks too."

"So we'll play in the ocean all day?"

"Sounds good to me." He winked, and the floor shifted underneath her feet.

Melene scolded herself. Aiden was off limits. She had to stop being so affected by every little smile or gesture he innocently directed her way. He seemed to have no idea how appealing he was, but staying immune to him was tougher than working fourteen-hour days in the hot sun to dig wells for villages.

"Let's do it." Since she was already in her swimming suit, she grabbed a water bottle from the fridge then went and brushed her teeth, reapplied tinted sunscreen moisturizer to her face, put on some cinnamon lip gloss, and refastened her hair in a ponytail. She was tempted to put on a little mascara, but not only would that give the wrong impression, it would probably just end up smudged and looking awful under her eyes. She slipped one of the lacy white swimsuit coverups over her head and walked through the main area.

Aiden was on the phone. He glanced at her and his gaze immediately stuck and turned searing. A spark lit in her chest, and she smiled at him.

His lips turned up in an appealing and heart-stopping smile, but then whoever he was on the phone with must've connected. He tilted his chin to her and started speaking rapidly into the phone. Someone must've interrupted him because he gave a soft laugh and repeated everything much slower. She smiled to herself. Jamaicans were very laid back, and though English was their national language, they had their own accent and slipped in Patois often. They probably had as hard of a time understanding Americans or British people as she did understanding them at times.

She walked back out to the patio, sat on a soft chair, and took in the gorgeous view of the infinity pool surrounded by flowers and greenery and the ocean below. The clear, blue sky was revealed through the leaves of the palm, mahogany, cedar, and lime trees. It smelled incredible here with the flowers, lime, and cedar scents combining with a salty twang from the ocean.

She waited for Aiden and mulled over the way he'd just looked at her. It frustrated her. He was the one who'd pulled her hands away from his chest and reminded her in no uncertain terms that they were temporary and would never work. Why did he keep giving her looks like that then? His friend Jace, back on the ship that first day, had referenced how women always went for him. Aiden either wasn't as innocent as she thought and he was messing with her head, or he was too innocent and women just pursued him because of how appealing and unassuming he was. She was pretty certain it was the latter, but she needed to keep her guard up if it was the former. She'd always trusted and liked the Deltas, but Aiden had been gone from Summit Valley for a long time and had probably been hardened by his time in the SEALs. Maybe he wasn't innocent at all, but playing her for all he was worth. Maybe it was entertainment or a distraction for him.

The door opened, and she shook off her worries and put a smile on her face. *Keep it temporary, keep it casual*, she reminded herself. Aiden was here on assignment and obviously wasn't willing to try for anything beyond hanging out together until the assignment was done.

She stood. "The beach?" she asked brightly.

"Yes, ma'am. The staff will deliver all the equipment with our lunch, so right now it's just relaxing and a swim race or two with yours truly."

She laughed at that. "You think I can win a swim race against Aquaman?"

He grinned and shrugged those beautiful shoulders of his. She wondered if he'd take his shirt off when they got to the water. She could finally glimpse that tattoo. "You can sure try."

"If only it could be a foot race," she said.

He lifted his eyebrows. "Maybe with all the years of training in the military, I could run as fast as the famed Melene Collier. How many state records do you still hold?"

"I don't know." She was flattered he'd remembered as he was a year older than her and already gone to the military her senior year when she'd really shattered records.

"I bet it's a lot. You still run?"

"As much as I can."

He nodded. "No wonder your legs are so perfect ... I mean ..." He trailed off as his eyes widened.

She appreciated the compliment, but they were back to the fact that he shouldn't have given it. She shook her head and started toward the beach path. Aiden grabbed a couple beach towels and caught up to her. Neither of them said anything as they walked down the trail to their own private paradise. If only ... nope, she couldn't think like that. Temporary. Good friends. Aquaman as her protector. It was all fine, and she was grateful for the safety of this beautiful spot and that Aiden was here for her.

Chapter Eight

Melene squished through the sand. She didn't have shoes on, and the soft squishiness felt great between her toes. Aiden dropped the towels on one of the beach chairs. She hadn't even noticed the two chairs in the dark last night. She looked around at their little sandy cove, marveling at the beautiful spot. There was a sheer rock ledge about a hundred feet to the left that made a natural border with the sand. A layer of thick trees and undergrowth obscured whatever was to the right. It looked like their own private jungle in that direction. She imagined as they swam out they'd be able to see the other villas' small beaches, if they all had them, the larger beach they'd landed on last night, and maybe even some of the rest of the resort. Was another resort to their left? She needed to get directions down. The sun was coming up above their villa, so that way was east. That meant the ocean was west and the rest of their resort was north of her. Okay. That helped settle her.

She turned to slip off her coverup and drop it on a chair. Aiden slid his shirt over his head. Suddenly, she wasn't settled at all. She was the furthest thing from settled. Stirred up, intrigued, drawn to, filled with a desire to look at and touch him.

They were close, close enough she could gape at the nicely formed muscles of his chest, abdomen, shoulders and arms, and even more importantly, she could clearly see the tattoo over his heart.

Aiden watched her with those penetrating blue eyes as she met his gaze, then dropped hers to study the tattoo in depth. It was two military dog tags crossed over each other with a trident behind them.

She stepped closer and read the names on the dog tags. Admiral Davidson Delta and SEAL Aiden Delta. Thankfully, not a woman.

She shouldn't have, but she softly touched his warm, taut skin and then let her fingers trail over the tattoo. Aiden sucked in a breath, but he didn't pull away and he didn't grab her hand and remove it from his chest like he had earlier.

"I like this," she said softly. "Papa Delta is amazing."

He smiled. "He is."

She flattened her palm against the muscle of his chest, covering the tattoo. His breath quickened as she eased her hand along his chest until the tattoo was revealed again. She loved touching him and if the fast thrumming of his heart and the warm look in his blue gaze was any indicator, he must have liked it too.

"You really are Aquaman. This is the second tattoo with a trident in it."

Winking, he said, "You can make that my nickname."

"I think I already have."

They stood there smiling at each other, and she had no idea how either of them was going to keep boundaries and remember this was temporary.

"You said you have one more tattoo. Can I see it?"

He slowly turned. Her hand was on his chest and she didn't lift it, so her fingers and palm dragged along the side of his shoulder and then to his back. As his back came into full view, she was as impressed as she'd been with his chest. Obviously he had to be fit to be a SEAL, but did he have to be so attractive she could only stare at him?

His broad back was defined with muscle and smooth, tanned skin. He obviously spent most of his time outside.

On his right shoulder blade were tattooed the words *Fear Not*, and below them *Isaiah 41:10*.

She touched this tattoo like she had the last one, but the fact that it was scripture helped her keep her wanton thoughts in line better. "Fear thou not; for I am with thee. Be not dismayed ..." she quoted.

He turned and caught her hand in his, pulling it to his heart. His blue eyes seared into her, her thoughts scattered, and she completely forgot the scripture. All she could see was Aiden Delta staring deeply at her with those blue eyes she could never get enough of. She felt his strong and accelerated heartbeat under their joined hands.

"... for I am thy God;" he picked up where she'd left off. "I will strengthen thee; yea, I will help thee; yea, I will uphold thee with the right hand of my righteousness."

Melene was completely caught up in this moment and this

man. She could easily fall for him. If only they had that chance. He seemed near perfect to her.

"I love that scripture," she admitted. "I used to repeat it when I was on my first missions and I felt so alone, missing home and my family and scared of ... far too many things."

"I don't like that you are scared." His blue gaze was far too penetrating.

She licked her lips and glanced away. What was there to say? She put herself in situations that most people wouldn't so she could serve and try to inspire and lift children and families to overcome hardship and get themselves out of their deprived circumstances. The Lord had protected her more times than she could count, most dramatically when this beautiful man rose out of the ocean a few days ago. She had faith and knew all things would come together for the good of those that loved God, but she still let fear overtake her at times.

He squeezed her hand, bringing her attention back to his handsome face. "I can relate to being afraid. There have been times during battles that I was sure I would be killed." His eyes darkened, but then they filled with light again as he admitted, "This scripture would be on repeat through my brain, and I'd just turn it all over to the Lord and fight to the very best of my abilities. If it was His will that I survived to fight another day, then I would."

Her chest was warm and she was so impressed by him. "That's a lot of faith." She realized it was true, though. Either one of them could be killed, no matter that they were trying to serve God and others. They had to go forward with faith and trust in His will.

He shrugged, his beautiful shoulders flexing. "I sometimes think this entire life is just a test of faith. When I can keep my faith strong, even if things aren't going the way I want at the moment, it all turns out the way it should. I've been able to let go of the fear, stress, and pain and turn it over to Him. He will always strengthen me, if I'll let him."

"I love that and you're right. Faith is a choice I have to make over and over again as well." She hadn't been in the extreme danger he'd been in, but she'd been in scary and heartbreaking situations and felt despair, fear, and heartache that only God could heal. It strengthened her own faith that the tough Navy SEAL could admit to the same feelings she'd experienced.

"As long as we keep making that choice," he said, "I think we'll be okay."

She nodded her agreement, but they both fell silent. The moment was sweet, tender, and far too intimate for her susceptible heart. Aiden Delta was the exact replica of the man she'd always dreamed would someday appear in her life ... and he'd already told her this was only temporary and made himself off limits.

Looking away, she had to find some way to distance herself or she'd be on her knees begging him to choose her like he chose faith. To not be afraid of where their relationship would go, but to trust it would all work out. She didn't know if she had that much faith and had no idea how to ask it of him.

She pulled her hand away and murmured, "Swimming first?"

"Yep."

He checked some things on his phone and she waited, unable to avoid staring at him. Then he secured his phone in his pocket, gave her an irresistible grin, picked her up off her feet, slid her over his shoulder, and ran for the ocean.

"Stop!" Melene cried out, laughing more in surprise than anything.

He only laughed at her. She bounced on his firm shoulder, and she was grateful all the nausea from being on ships was gone or she would've been in trouble.

His hands on her legs and back felt far too good, but her abdomen digging into his shoulder wasn't comfortable. Thank heavens for the discomfort so she could stop being so sappily drawn to him.

He pushed through until he was waist deep in the calm ocean, and then he lifted her off his shoulder and tossed her into the air.

Melene cried out in surprise again. She hit the water and luckily closed her mouth so she didn't swallow the salty ocean.

She came up sputtering and laughing. Aiden was right there, grinning at her. "Again?" he asked.

"No." She shook her head, but she couldn't stop laughing. "I'm not some child you can just throw around."

He grinned. "You're as light as a child."

"I am a woman," she reminded him. "You *have* to remember that."

His gaze swept over her as it had many times, and she didn't know if she could handle all the conflicting messages he kept sending her. Did he want distance or not? "There's no way I'd forget that."

He cupped the water and she thought he'd splash her, but he splashed his own face and rubbed at it as if he were shaking something off. He gave her a lopsided grin. "Swim race?"

"Oh, my. As if I could win a swim race with Aquaman."

"Do you remember when I used to teach you and your friends in the lake back home?"

She nodded. She remembered everything about him. "But even those incredible tips won't help me today."

His lips pursed as he studied her. He obviously wanted to race, or maybe he simply wanted something to distract them both from the intense emotion that surrounded them and seemed to burst into an unquenchable flame with any look, touch, or word that may or may not have been intended for such a purpose. Whew. This was going to be a long time waiting to be safe from that jerk General Phillip if she and Aiden couldn't rein in the longing and respect that kept growing between them. At least it was apparent he felt it too, but he seemed to be better at fighting it or redirecting.

"I'll use only my arms," he declared.

"We'll see if that even helps me." His arms were so strong she doubted she'd have any advantage.

"To the rocks over there and back." He pointed to the left about a hundred feet.

She nodded, then she took off with a basic freestyle stroke. He laughed from behind her, as if her cheating was hilarious and wouldn't even help her. He was probably right. She tried to put her face in the water to swim more efficiently like her instructors had taught her in junior lifeguarding and Aiden had helped her with back in that cold mountain lake, but then she realized she was going at an angle out into the ocean. She kept her head up for a few more strokes.

She could hear Aiden coming behind her, and then he blew

past her. She stopped swimming, treaded water, and simply watched him go. He wasn't kicking his legs, but his upper body was so strong and efficient that he glided through the water like some kind of machine.

He reached the rocks, turned underwater using only his arms, and flew back toward her. He stopped in front of her and blinked the water out of his eyes as he treaded water. "What was that? I didn't think you'd concede I was the champion so easily."

She laughed. "That was impressive. I guess you are Aquaman."

"And a Navy SEAL."

"Lest I forget." She squinted at the rocks, the warm sun kissing her forehead. "It's no competition unless we make it harder."

"Okay. I'll just use my legs."

She tilted her head. "Will that even slow you down?"

"For sure."

She pointed back toward the shore. "You start over there and you only can do the dolphin kick, like the one in that hard stroke, the um ..."

"Butterfly?" His blue eyes glinted at her as if she'd just given him an advantage.

"Yeah," she said. She would probably lose horribly again, but it was fun trying.

"Sounds good." He swam off toward the beach, cruising like he had a motor as he used both his arms and legs.

Melene turned from staring at him and took off toward the rocks. She wasn't one to cheat, but she needed any advantage she could get.

She was getting close to the rocks and he hadn't reached her yet. She had to get all the way back to the beach, though.

Something large swam underneath her. Melene cried out and almost kicked whatever it was, but as she glanced through the clear water, she could see it was Aiden. His arms were pinned at his sides. His lower body moved like a dolphin and he was gliding quickly toward the rocks. What a showoff.

Melene went underwater and grabbed one of his legs before he was out of reach. It almost ripped from her grasp, but she clamped on and he dragged her a few feet before he stopped. They both surfaced, and she had to release his leg or she'd be dragged back under. He laughed and shook his head at her.

"I didn't figure my benevolent woman for such a cheater."

She flushed at the possessive pronoun.

"I didn't figure my hot Aquaman for such a showoff."

He brushed his hand through his short hair and all those lovely muscles flexed. "Really?" He winked.

She splashed water at him. He laughed and then he grabbed her around the waist and lifted her up into the air, keeping them both above the surface with only his legs moving.

She laughed. "You are some kind of mutant. I think you *are* Aquaman."

He only smiled at that and slid her back into the water, unfortunately releasing her. "Okay. Let's try one more. Race back to the beach and I'll only use my left arm."

"Left arm? No legs at all?"

"Nope."

She laughed. "You'll still smoke me."

"We'll see."

91

She swam as fast as she could toward the beach. Within seconds he'd reached her, using only his left arm. Sheesh. He was impressive and a lot of fun.

They could keep playing in the water today and maybe she'd be able to stay strong and keep some distance. But probably not.

Chapter Nine

Aiden had a lot of fun playing in the water with Melene most of the day. His sensors worked well even in the water, informing him when room service arrived at lunchtime. He still checked the cameras and their surroundings vigilantly.

They did more swim races and then he worked with her on swimming technique, which turned out to be a mistake with the whole keeping his distance thing, but was a lot of fun for his heart and body wanting to be closer to Melene.

After they ate lunch up at the villa, they brought all the equipment the staff had left and spent hours kayaking, paddle boarding, trying to do headstands and yoga on the paddle boards, snorkeling, and finally he took her on some very short scuba dives. He didn't dare be too far from the beach. Though everything seemed quiet and he had no idea how General Phillip would find them here, he had to make sure he didn't forget what he was doing here.

Forgetting would be all too easy with the alluring and fun

Melene within arm's reach all day. They had a lot of fun together. On the ships traveling here, she'd been sick but so sweet and had impressed him with her patience and grit. Today she'd been fun, teasing, and still so sweet and had impressed him with her ability to have fun and banter. If he was a normal guy with a normal job, he'd be proposing already.

Sadly, he wasn't.

They hardly used any of the oxygen in the scuba tanks, so when they finished on the beach, they stowed the kayaks and paddle boards by the beach chairs and then piled the snorkel and scuba equipment on the laydown chairs. They could use it all again tomorrow. Today had been great. Aiden rarely got this much playtime and having it not only in the ocean but with Melene was a dream come true.

He assumed the plan would be similar tomorrow, but already he was concerned about how long he could keep going like this. If he and Melene spent many more days in this tropical spot of paradise, there was no way he could stay strong and keep his distance. As it was, he'd laughed with her and touched her far too much. He'd told her this morning it was temporary and they couldn't be together. How could he keep that in mind?

They headed to their separate rooms to shower and even the sweet smile and thank you for a fun day she gifted him with before she closed her bedroom door had his heart racing and him longing to never leave her side again.

Whew. He was acting like a smitten sap. Worse than how Thor acted around Shelly.

Before he showered, he checked everything and then looked at the messages on his phone. Papa had nothing new but said Sheriff

Reed had heard some men were quietly asking around Summit Valley about Melene's family. They'd disappeared before he could find them, but he had deputies watching out for Melene's family.

Jace texted him, just checking in, telling him it was boring without him. That made him smile.

Thor texted, wondering if Aiden was still ugly and promising he could be his best man no matter how ugly he was. That made him laugh but also feel a tug toward home and his family. He hadn't planned on making the wedding, so it shouldn't hurt that he was less likely now to get there than he had been a week ago.

He showered and dressed in the nicest clothes he had, a button-down short-sleeved white shirt and khaki pants, strapping on his pistol and pocketing his knife and phone. He brushed his teeth, sprayed on some cologne, brushed his hair, and should've cursed himself for making such an effort. He'd told Melene they wouldn't work, and he'd meant it.

He brushed at his hair with his hand. Before he could second guess his intentions or give himself a stern warning to keep his hands off, he walked out of his room. The main room was empty. The sun was still a couple hours from setting. It had been a fun day in the sun and the water.

Fun. Protection. Doing his job to keep Melene safe. That was enough. It had to be enough.

His phone beeped. He pulled it out and saw the golf cart from the resort approaching. A young man left the food on the front porch table, picked up the lunch dishes, rapped on the door, and drove off. Aiden checked each camera angle for what felt like the hundredth time today, but there was nothing else stirring anywhere close to the villa. It was more difficult being a one-man protection detail and the fact that Melene was so fun and attractive couldn't sidetrack him.

Opening the door, he retrieved the tray. It smelled delicious, like savory meat and yeasty bread. Closing the door with his foot, he balanced the tray on the entry table and re-armed the security before lifting the tray again and walking into the open main area. Melene's door opened and the most beautiful sight he'd ever seen in his life walked out. He almost dropped the tray of food.

He wanted to say something poetic. He wanted to chuck the food and rush over and pull her close, but he simply stared at her. Her smooth, beautiful skin, dark eyes, and full lips were enhanced with light makeup. Her long, dark hair curled down her back and trailed over one perfect shoulder. Her pale blue dress outlined all the womanly curves that seemed even more pronounced by how thin she was. He loved that she wasn't trying to be thin, but she worked so hard for the children in the heat that she struggled to keep weight on. She was genuine and so true to herself. She tucked her hair behind her ear and shyly smiled at him.

"You look amazing, Aiden," she said.

Dang. She'd said it first. He tilted his chin up and tried to play it cool, but there was nothing cool about him right now. He was on fire. For her. "You are the most beautiful woman I've ever seen, Melene," he said far too huskily.

Her smile grew.

His phone beeped a warning.

Aiden's eyes widened. He hurriedly set the food on the dining room table, then yanked his phone out as he returned to the entryway. Melene tried to follow him. He held up his hand to hold her back. Clicking on the cameras and sensors, he couldn't see anything for a moment. He'd let himself get distracted.

Transferring his phone to his left hand, he jerked his pistol out and cocked it. He could hear Melene's quick breaths behind him. He wanted to reassure her, but he had to figure out what was out there first.

He found the heat signature behind some trees and willed the person to move so he could catch them on the cameras and see if it was a worker pruning trees and he was overreacting or if it was a paid mercenary who'd somehow found them. They hadn't interacted with anyone outside the Navy sailors who'd dropped them off here. He supposed one of the Navy men or women could've taken the million-dollar bribe and revealed they saw them get off a ship near Jamaica, but he thought they'd done a good job of hiding their faces. Could a security camera have captured an angle of Melene's face and a resort guard sold them out?

The heat signature moved and he let out a relieved laugh.

"What?" Melene pressed into his back and suddenly there was a very different worry as her smooth curves filled him with desire. "What is it?"

"A deer," Aiden admitted, showing her the video. He slid his Glock back into the holster, his phone into his pocket, and turned to her. She was so close, and so beautiful. He hadn't been bothered by her smell at all when she was sick and claimed she didn't smell great, but right now she smelled fabulous, like sweet mint and flowers. He *was* bothered by how alluring she was. It bothered him a lot.

"We'd better eat before it gets cold," he rushed out before he hauled her close and tasted her lips first and then explored her slender neck.

"Okay." She stepped back, but there was a disappointment in her dark eyes that dug at him. She swept toward the table.

He followed her and picked up the tray of food. "Do you want to eat out back?"

"Sure." She grabbed water bottles from the fridge and he waited for her to walk in front of him out onto the patio.

They sat by the sparkling pool with the gorgeous scenery of greenery, flowers, and the ocean below. The food was delicious, and they chatted about their families as they ate. She wanted to hear all about his twin Thor and his fiancée Shelly, their upcoming wedding, and he even shared Thor's funny text. Melene, of course, worried that she was keeping him from the wedding. He reassured her wouldn't have been able to make it anyway.

Dinner was finished and cleaned up. She excused herself and went into her bedroom. Aiden hurried into his own bathroom, brushed his teeth, but stopped himself from spritzing on more cologne. He stared at himself in the mirror, his own blue eyes questioning. What was he doing? He'd never struggled like this, but Melene was so incredible. They could talk about anything and nothing. She was fun to play around with in the water, charitable and kind, and the most appealing woman he'd ever met.

He did his routine checks, almost wishing some mercenary would show up to distract him, passed a hand over his face, and walked back out. It was only eight o'clock. He couldn't hide out in his room all night.

Melene walked out as well and inclined her head toward the beach. "Walk down on the beach?" she asked.

"Sure." He should've suggested they play a card game or watch an action movie or something that wouldn't be romantic. He couldn't seem to help himself from wanting to be alone with Melene in romantic spots.

They walked out the back patio door and he barely restrained himself from taking her hand or putting his hand on the small of her back. Slowly making their way down the beach path, she tripped on her heels and he had no choice but to wrap his arm around her waist.

She stared up at him, her lips soft and full and her beguiling dark eyes sparkling at him. "Thanks," she said, sounding out of breath and looking as if she wanted nothing more than to kiss him.

"Sure." His gaze trailed over her beautiful face and his hands had a mind of their own as they slid along the soft skin of her back.

He saw the pulse point in her neck thud quicker and he felt his own heart racing out of control. He wanted to kiss her. Desperately. But he'd been the idiot who said nothing could happen between them. Getting involved was dangerous to the mission, wasn't fair to her, and it would devastate him when he had to walk away.

Aiden used self-control honed from his upbringing and his years in the military and he thought even his drill sergeant from BUD/S training would be proud of him for stepping back and releasing her. It was harder than not ringing the bell, that was for sure.

He gestured her down the last few stairs. Her face reflected the loss of the moment and a sharp disappointment. He clenched his fist so he wouldn't reach out for her again.

She walked onto the beach and slid her strappy heels off, leaving them in the sand. Aiden couldn't tear his eyes away from her. Had there ever been a woman as captivating as this one? Not that he'd ever met.

As she straightened, they were face to face and Aiden's heart was thudding out of control. He tried to remember all the reasons he needed to keep his distance and stay strong, but his mind was suddenly blank of anything but Melene.

The fact was the three-quarters moon was giving off a romantic light, the lapping of the waves and the delicious smell of Melene and most of all the sweetness and appeal of her face, her body, and her very soul wrapped around him. He had no power to resist when she made the first move. She shifted closer, placed her lovely hands on his chest and then slowly, tantalizingly, she slid her hands across his chest, over his shoulders, and then around his neck.

Luckily, Aiden could hold his breath for over three minutes because there was no oxygen getting through to his lungs at the moment.

His arms naturally wrapped her up tight and his fingers and palms caressed the warm skin of her back. She was tantalizing. He was in so much trouble right now, but he couldn't have cared less. He was ringing the bell and giving up his will ... to Melene. He had no idea how a mighty sailor had fallen so quickly, no idea how to navigate a future with her, and at the moment he didn't care.

"Melene ..." Her name came out in a moan.

She smiled up at him, blinking her long lashes at him. "Yes, Aquaman?"

Aiden groaned and bent down. Just one sweet kiss and then he'd apologize for his weakness and somehow regain his strength, distance, and priorities.

A splashing and the sound of voices yanked him from his besotted state and away from Melene's intoxicating draw.

Aiden spun and held Melene behind him, trying to discern where the sound was coming from, how close it was, and why his alarms hadn't gone off.

Melene leaned close to him, but to her credit she didn't cry out or ask questions, seeming to feel the tenseness radiating from him.

Another splash and his gaze was drawn to the south. The moon illuminated a small canoe with two boys manning it. They were smoothly rowing around the cliffs and chattering to each other.

Aiden relaxed slightly. Just a couple of kids out on a ride at night. They were probably sneaking out and thinking they were rebels. He remembered that feeling well with all of his and Thor's escapades, sturdy tricks, and a few activities that would've landed them in a juvenile detention center if they'd been caught. Thankfully, they hadn't.

He pulled out his phone and checked, but everything was quiet around the villa. He turned slightly and sheltered Melene with his arm. "Just a couple of boys."

She smiled up at him. "Boys are the best."

His stomach lifted like he was speeding down a roller coaster. Was he the best? He was a boy. A man, but around her he felt like a boy with his first crush. "What about men?" he asked huskily. "In particular, Aquaman."

Her smile grew and she cuddled in closer to him, one hand cupping his jawline. Her touch and the look in her eyes made his pulse take off. "Aquaman is the very, very best of all men," she whispered, leaning up.

Aiden wanted nothing more than to kiss her long and slow, but the splashing and the voices were growing dangerously close. He had to keep his head on straight. The two boys were most likely no danger and wouldn't expose them, but Aiden was taking no risks with this beautiful woman who was consuming him and becoming his entire world no matter how valiantly he claimed to be fighting these feelings.

He ushered her back across the beach. "Hold that thought," he murmured. He would get her back to the villa. Set all the alarms. Then he was going to show her exactly how her Aquaman would kiss her. Hang the consequences, their callings in life, and his own fears that their relationship would implode worse than Jake and Charisse's had.

To his surprise, Melene ducked under his arm and hurried to the water's edge.

"What are you doing?" he asked, rushing to catch her before the boys saw her.

"I haven't been around children in almost a week," she explained. "Can't we say hello?"

"No." He shook his head. "What if they recognize you?"

She looked at him as if he'd lost his mind. "No way would those innocent boys know about some million-dollar bounty."

Aiden was not taking any risks. He swept her off the ground

and against his chest, burying her face into his shoulder. "It's not worth risking," he ground out.

"'ello?" a young voice called. "Whatcha doin' to the lady?"

Aiden pivoted, hiding her from the boys. "She's my lady," he said to them as the canoe got far too close for comfort and then they rammed their small craft into the beach. Those two were fast. "I'm taking her home."

Melene pulled from his shoulder, and though he could've physically prevented her from moving, he didn't want to be some brute and control her. "I am not your lady," she shot at him. "You told me yourself we couldn't get involved."

Aiden tensed. This was no time to get into that discussion.

"Yo, mon." The boys scrambled out of the boat and marched right up to them. They couldn't have been more than seven or eight, scrawny and cute and full of fire, even though neither of them measured above his waist. He had a flashback to him and Thor thinking they were bigger than their britches when they were around seven, telling a couple of teenage boys to stop bullying Bentley Jardine, and gotten beaten up for their intervention. At their begging, Papa had never said anything to their parents or the boys' parents, but he'd agreed to up their hand-to-hand training.

"You no hurt the lady," the smaller one demanded.

"Oh my goodness, you're adorable." Melene clapped her hands together in delight. "I'm Mel—"

"Melissa," Aiden interrupted. Did she honestly have no worries of General Phillip finding them? He'd gotten the impression Melene was smart and savvy to the ways of the world, but apparently children caused her to throw any caution out the window.

Kind of like her smile, dark eyes, and warm touch throws all your self restraint out the window?

He tried to shake that thought off, but it was sadly true.

Melene looked up at him, her own eyes full of fire. "Yes, Aquaman, that's right. Melissa. Now put me down please so I can talk to my new friends."

Aiden rolled his eyes, heaved out a disgruntled breath, and let her feet slide to the sand. She immediately sank to her knees so she was on the boys' level.

"How are you handsome guys doing?" she asked, all sweet and perfect and far too naïve.

"We're *irie*," the spokesman said, pronouncing it ahy-ree. Aiden always enjoyed hearing local slang.

"What are your names?"

"I'm Ace, and this here is Dante," the taller of the two said. "Is the tough guy hurting you?"

"Oh no, sweetheart." Melene blinked up at him. "No. He's my hero, actually."

The boys both nodded and one put a fist out to Aiden to bump. He bumped it, but he wanted to end this interaction no matter how sweet and innocent it seemed.

"That's *irie*." Dante smiled, showing several missing teeth.

"And what are you tough guys doing on the ocean by yourselves at night?" Melene still looked happy as sunshine to see them, but she obviously didn't want them in danger. Forget that she might be placing herself there.

"We're gonna fish, mon. No worries," Ace drawled out. He

looked her over. "You the prettiest lady I have *ever* seen. Are you famous?"

Melene let out a peal of tinkling and beautiful laughter. "No, sweetie. I'm not at all famous."

"Ya sure? Your face is so beautiful, I think I musta seen it in ma dreams." He winked. "Or you're a movie star."

Melene laughed again, but the boys were studying her far too intently and Aiden's senses were tingling. They'd seen her face somewhere. Maybe they'd seen the bounty and a picture on some device, or maybe Phillip was circulating posters and flyers to every remote spot of the world at this point. Who knew? Aiden had to get her out of here. How soon could Papa relocate them? He didn't want to go it on his own, but he might have to.

"Mel ... Melissa. We've got to go." He didn't want to raise their suspicions further.

"Just a moment, Aquaman." Her sweet smile was irresistible, but he had to resist it. These boys might be no danger at all, but he couldn't count on that. He was itching to call Papa and make some quick and smart decisions. Much smarter than when he'd almost kissed her. What an idiot he'd been.

"Yo, Aquaman?" Ace asked. "You don't have all the tats or long hairs."

Aiden shook his head and would've smiled if he wasn't so concerned. They were seriously cute kids.

"But he swims faster than Aquaman," Melene confided in them.

"Sweet," Ace said. He looked back at Melene. "I got it. You're the lady from Mission Impossible."

"Thandie Newton," Aiden said before he could stop himself. He focused on Melene's beautiful face. "She does look like her."

"But you're not her?" Dante asked, obviously disappointed not to be meeting a famous actress.

"Sorry, no." Melene shook her head.

"And we've got to go." Aiden tried for a stern look.

Melene nodded as if resigned to listen to him. She stood and then bent and gave each of the boys a hug. "It was wonderful to meet you both, Ace and Dante," she said warmly.

"You too, beautiful." They climbed back into their boat and Aiden shoved them off.

They both waved and set off, paddling and chattering again.

Aiden turned and wrapped his hand around Melene's elbow, directing her to the stairs. She paused to pick up her shoes.

"Sorry. They were just so cute I had to say hi," she said as they walked up the stairs.

"We have to be vigilant and keep anyone from seeing your beautiful face," he said, feeling a little chagrined but still concerned. If she would've been feisty or angry at him, it would've been easier to reprimand her about being safe.

"They thought I was an actress," she said. "I've never seen Mission Impossible, but I remember Thandie Newton from Pursuit of Happyness with Will Smith. She's a beautiful lady."

Aiden wanted to tell Melene she was more beautiful, but this wasn't the time to flirt.

"The boys didn't recognize *me*," she insisted.

"Who knows?" Aiden's mind was spinning. They walked past the pool and into the house. He released her arm, secured the patio door, and checked to make sure all the alarms were armed.

"I've got to call Papa and see what he thinks. We're going to have to relocate."

Melene's eyes registered alarm. "I apologize, Aiden. I didn't realize talking to children could compromise us."

He looked her over. The main area was dimly lit, and she was gorgeous. To him, she was prettier than any famous actress. "It's all right. It's probably fine, but I'm not risking it. Please get some sleep and I'll wake you as soon as I'm ready to move."

She nodded, but instead of turning to her bedroom, she strode to him, stood on tiptoes, and kissed his cheek. "Thank you for watching over me," she whispered against his cheek. "I'm sorry if I made it harder."

Aiden closed his eyes so he couldn't be taken in by her incredible beauty, but there was no way to shut off his other senses. She smelled like heaven and her soft lips on his cheek messed with his mind.

"It's okay," he managed, meeting her gaze because his mom didn't raise any wimps. "Get some rest. I'll wake you up when I'm ready to relocate."

"Thanks." She smiled up at him, but her dark eyes seemed ... disappointed. Had she wanted that kiss on the beach as much as he had?

She turned and walked slowly into her bedroom. Aiden watched her go. She gave him one last look over her shoulder and he almost rushed after her and gathered her to him. He stood still and as soon as she disappeared, he pulled out his phone.

Distancing himself was the best idea right now. It was good the boys had interrupted that kiss, but he felt achy and like he had the flu. He wanted to kiss her far too much. What had happened to all his supposed self-control?

He pushed a number and barked out, "Papa, we've got a situation."

As he outlined what had happened and he and Papa discussed every possibility and different ideas for what to do, he paced the living area. He had to focus on protecting Melene. If he let his mind wander back to kissing her, he'd make a mess of everything and worst of all, probably endanger her.

Her safety was all that mattered.

Maybe someday, after all of this was over, they could ...

He couldn't let his mind go there. The answer to a future with Melene was still no.

Chapter Ten

Melene could not sleep. She stretched out in the comfortable bed in a tank top and shorts and listened to Aiden's low rumbling voice in the other room. She couldn't make out all the words clearly—it depended which way he was pacing at that moment—but he was obviously concerned about her interaction with the boys and trying to figure out the safest and quickest way to relocate.

She felt awful that she'd caused him stress because of a simple exchange with two cuties. Her head had been a muddled mess before the boys arrived. She'd been so close to Aiden kissing her and then suddenly he spun away and moved to protect her.

When she saw those two adorable little boys, relief had rushed through her that there was no danger and it felt like coming home. A close second to the comfort of being in Aiden's arms, but none of the tingles. Interacting with children from around the world was what she did, and she couldn't believe those sweet, undersized boys who'd been willing to stand up to the likes of the tough Aiden to protect her could pose any danger to her. Aiden obviously thought they did.

She realized he wasn't talking anymore, and then she heard the fridge open and close. Seconds later, his footsteps came past her bedroom door and she heard movement in his room.

Sliding out of bed, she wondered if it was smart to approach him. She justified she needed to know if they were moving so she could pack, but she didn't care about even having a toothbrush compared to her need to be in Aiden's arms.

They'd been so close to that kiss, and she'd wanted nothing more. Yet she sensed nothing had changed regarding their future. Once the mission was done, Aiden would go back to his life and she'd go back to hers. That was how it was supposed to be and how it should be. They both knew it wasn't smart to get emotionally invested. They both had their purposes and paths in life. They both couldn't afford to fall in love.

It was too late. She clenched her hands and gave a grunt of frustration. She'd like to meet a woman strong enough to not fall for the likes of Aiden Delta. It was going to crush her when they parted. It was going to rip her apart and she would never be the same. She was too far gone to care or focus on future fears and pain right now. She wanted to kiss him and forget about all the other worries. She chose to have faith in so many areas of her life. Why couldn't she have faith that the Lord would help them be together if it was His will? Yet she wasn't sure if her need to kiss and be close to Aiden was motivated by heaven's nudges or her own selfish desires.

She crept out of her room and into the doorway of his. The

light from his bathroom illuminated him. He shoved a few more things into his large bag and then strapped it shut.

"Aiden." His name came out as a breathy sigh.

He spun and she could see how taut his body was, the angst radiating from him.

Melene was done being strong, done fighting the need for him. She ran into his room and collided with him.

"Melene." His voice was husky and full of her. His bag dropped to the floor and his arms wrapped around her.

She threw her arms around his neck and rushed out, "I'm sorry if I caused you trouble with those boys." She stared into his brilliantly blue eyes, wanting to know his deepest feelings. He cared for her, but was it enough to risk an uncertain, difficult and probably doomed to failure long-distance relationship?

"It'll be okay," he said. He hugged her close. She wasn't sure if it was to reassure her or because it felt as incredible to him as it did to her to be entangled in each other's arms. "Papa is sending Thor and Greer on a chartered jet. A man he trusts is coming for us in about an hour and will take us to meet them. Can you grab anything you need? I'll find a bag to put it in."

"I'm putting more of the Deltas out. I'm so sorry." She clung to him, praying he wouldn't let her go. She needed his protection, but most of all, she needed him. "What if Thor misses his wedding?"

He cracked a smile at that. "Somebody will come take his place with us if we get close to that. I'm not risking Shelly's wrath for stealing her man."

She smiled. "A Delta man isn't one you want to lose." Sadly, she didn't have this Delta man and probably never would. "Especially Aquaman," she said softly, though she should've left it alone.

"Ah, Melene." Her name came out as a rough breath.

Their gazes caught and she could see the longing deep in his eyes. She suddenly couldn't stand the ache for him one second longer. Before he could remind her they could never be together, before she could stew about all the reasons she needed to be strong, before she could allow fear to override faith, she arched up and pressed her lips to his.

If he was startled by her boldness, Aiden didn't show it. He didn't miss a beat. His mouth returned the pressure she'd initiated. They were instantly entangled in the most incredible kiss of her life. He maneuvered her mouth in a firm but tender kiss that had her tingling from head to toe. His hands ran up her back and he framed her face, tilting her head and deepening the kiss. Melene moaned and happily encouraged him to take the kiss to the next level.

She'd known kissing Aiden would be off the charts, but even her longings and visions hadn't created this.

A beep sounded from somewhere far too close.

Aiden jerked away from her and yanked out his phone. He looked at something for a few seconds. His brow furrowed and his body tightened reflexively. He pressed another couple of buttons on his phone and slung his bag over his shoulder, saying in a rush into his phone when it connected, "They're here. We're moving out now." He paused, then told whoever was on the line, "We can't wait, and circling around the resort is too risky. I'll be in contact with our location."

Horror rushed through Melene. Her gut tightened and her pulse raced. "Who's here?" she whispered back.

Aiden shoved his phone in an inside pocket of his bag without saying goodbye, zipped the top, cinched the straps, and took her hand. "Heat signatures approaching from the front."

"How many?"

"Dozens."

Melene's eyes widened. Had her little buddies ratted her out? More importantly, how on earth could she and Aiden escape?

Aiden said nothing as he hurried her through the main area and out the rear patio door, sliding it quietly shut behind them. They rushed across the pool area and down the trail. She had no shoes on and hadn't grabbed her stuff. No toothbrush. Again. She almost laughed at that errant thought. What did her breath matter if dozens of men were going to gun them down?

Aiden hadn't pulled the pistol off his hip. Did he have more guns in his bag? Would they set up resistance down at the beach or somehow hide out until Papa Delta's guy or Thor and Greer came? No way would that work. They couldn't hold off dozens of men.

Her heart beat so fast and her throat was so dry she couldn't even swallow to ask. She didn't dare say anything and risk giving away their position. As it was, she feared their quiet footsteps would lead the men to them.

She prayed desperately in her head as she and Aiden reached the beach. Had she signed this amazing man's death warrant? Would she soon be the property of the depraved General Phillip? No matter how tough, brave, and experienced Aiden was she saw no way to escape and no hope of rescue.

Chapter Eleven

Chills filled Melene and she trembled with fear. Aiden gave her a reassuring squeeze of the hand. She hated that he could see how terrified she was. She didn't want him to worry about her when he needed to be focused on their escape.

He released her and slid off his shoes, socks, and shirt, hiding them under some bushes. He sorted through the scuba gear resting on the beach chair. He handed her the face mask she'd worn today, shoved the other face mask on top of his head, and then picked up both air tanks and regulators, hefting one in each hand. His muscles bulged, and he truly looked like Aquaman right now. He slipped one pair of flippers through a couple of his fingers.

He sped across the beach, but slowed his steps as he entered the water. Melene followed close behind, knowing it was her only option. Aiden was her safe spot, and he would protect her from whatever was coming. Had those darling boys truly shared her location for a million dollars? It seemed unfathomable, but they had to be the source, even if they'd told someone about her and Aiden innocently. There wasn't any other option that she could see.

The lukewarm water closed over her ankles and then her calves. She stayed right close to Aiden, fear coating her in an icy sweat. It was obvious he was planning to use the scuba gear to escape. He'd helped her do a few very short dives in shallow water earlier today. She was by no means accomplished at using the gear or confident in her abilities. There had been some moments when she'd breathed easily under the water and enjoyed the view under the sea of fish and plants. She hadn't told him earlier, but water had leaked in the side of her mask and filled her nose the third time they'd gone under. It had scared her. She'd been relieved when he'd brought her up and wasn't sure if scuba was for her.

As fast as she was breathing, she'd probably hyperventilate one foot into the ocean. She prayed desperately for their safety from whoever was coming and for her to please, please calm down. She was going to give away their location, get them both captured, or drown. She wasn't sure which option was worst at the moment, but she didn't want to endanger Aiden and she trusted him completely. Somehow, he'd help her through this.

She was waist deep in the water when Aiden turned to her. He took off his bag and set it in the water, then slid into the flippers and eased one of the oxygen tanks onto his back before loosening the straps on his bag and securing it over the tank. It barely fit.

Listening for someone pursuing them, she thought she heard footsteps but wasn't certain. Her pulse raced far too fast. Fear of so many things—being caught and taken to that awful General

Phillip; Aiden being hurt or killed; her drowning as they tried to scuba dive to safety—made her muscles tense up.

She watched as Aiden lifted the other tank and started sliding it onto her back. It was much, much heavier than she remembered. Had he put it on her while she was deeper in the water last time? Earlier, she'd been pretty focused on Aiden's fingers and palms brushing her bare skin. Right now, even that sensation couldn't distract her.

Suddenly, the ledge above them exploded in an awful cacophony of light and gunfire. Huge search lights penetrated through the trees and she could hear their villa being desecrated by what sounded like a hundred machine guns.

Melene jumped and bit her lip to not cry out. Aiden ignored the assault and secured her oxygen tank, adjusted the mask over her eyes and nose, making sure her hair wasn't caught in it—he'd told her earlier her hair could make it leak—and then he handed her the regulator.

He leaned close to her ear and said over the noise coming from above, "Remember to expel the air first before you take your first breath. I'll be right beside you."

She could not do this. She wanted to scream in horror and frustration. Aiden nodded to her and put his own face mask on. He took her hand and edged her deeper into the water.

The bullets stopped as quickly as they had begun. Eerie silence filled the air as the echoes died, and Aiden paused. She wasn't certain if he wanted to hear what was going on or if he didn't want to splash and give away their location.

"Melene Collier," an accented voice from the far side of the villa said through what sounded like a bullhorn. "Please step outside the front door with your hands up and we will not kill your protection. Your guard is to stay safely in the house."

Melene's eyes widened behind her mask. Aiden squeezed her hand, showed her how to push the button to expel the air, gently maneuvered the regulator into her mouth, and then tugged her into the ocean.

The lukewarm water closed over her head and Melene should've felt reassured that they were hidden from the mercenaries, but she was so terrified she couldn't calm down. Aiden held on to her hand and pulled her in until dark water enclosed her. The pressure of the water and lack of visibility felt like a tomb. The ocean was not welcoming her gently tonight. She pushed out a breath as hard as she could and then took quick panting breaths in and out. She felt herself getting lightheaded and confused. There was pressure on her head and ears, and she couldn't get enough oxygen.

Aiden was quickly swimming them through the ocean. She had no clue which direction, but her eyes adjusted and she could see the mass of dark ocean floor not a foot below her. How deep were they? How far did they have to go? Was she going to pass out from the lack of oxygen?

Water trickled in from the side of her mask and her nose was suddenly filled with water. It was too much. She was going to drown.

A dark, long shape slid past her right side. Melene screamed out, filled her mouth with salty water, and panic overwhelmed her. She ripped her hand from Aiden's, shoved off the bottom with her right foot, and a few seconds later burst out of the water.

She ripped her regulator out and her mask off and took gasping breaths of real air.

Aiden was instantly by her side.

"I can't," she gasped out, tasting salt water and trying to blow the water out that had filled her nose.

He put a hand over her mouth and tilted his head. They hadn't even rounded the cliffs to the south. The villa and all the lights were far too close. She could hear men shouting and running.

"You've got this," he whispered into her ear. "You're the bravest, toughest woman I know. Take slow breaths in the regulator."

"My mask is leaking," she squeaked back.

"It's all right." He gently adjusted it back over her eyes and nose, tightening the straps slightly. "If you're worried, push your free hand against the side that's leaking and it'll stop."

He didn't let her second guess it, but depressed the regulator and then put it back in her mouth. "Push the air out," he cautioned, and then he tugged her back under. The dark prison of water surrounded her again on every side.

Melene usually loved the ocean, but right now it was horrifying. She forced herself to push the air out hard and then she tried to draw in a very slow but not very calm breath, while holding on to her mask with her free hand so it didn't leak again.

Aiden's grip on her hand was tight and reassuring and he tugged her through the water, his strong legs and the fins doing all the work. Melene focused on clinging to his hand, pushing out a breath, and then pulling the next breath in as slowly as she could. It was disconcerting that she couldn't see much more than the ocean floor below them and occasionally a fish swimming by. Thankfully, no more large shapes swam by and her mask didn't leak with her holding it.

Trust Aiden, trust Aiden, she alternated repeating with desperate prayers that they would somehow survive.

She gradually realized that like earlier today when they'd messed around with scuba gear, she was doing it. She was breathing underwater. This afternoon it had been a cool novelty. Tonight it was the difference between life and death.

Her breathing calmed significantly, though the pressure on her head, ears, and sinuses wasn't going away. She figured she could live with that, but she did try to wiggle her jaw and then pinch her nose and blow out hard to pop her ears. It helped.

She alternated prayers of gratitude with prayers for protection. She tried to kick her legs and help out, but her efforts felt feeble and didn't seem to matter much as Aiden efficiently motored them through the ocean.

It was dark and murky, and she'd never been so scared in her life, but she kept praying and breathing and clinging to Aiden. She had no clue how much time had passed when she realized the pressure on her head was lightening, but the water was significantly colder. They seemed to change directions, and then it felt like they were swimming against a current. Not that it slowed Aiden down much. He probably didn't even need the fins.

Time passed, but she had no clue how much. Without being able to see and in the alien world of the ocean, or maybe a river at this point, she was completely out of her element.

She drew in a breath and no oxygen came. Blowing out slowly, she tried again with the same outcome. Her stomach flipped over, and panic filled her lungs instead of the air she needed. She tugged at Aiden's hand and yanked up, bursting out of the water much quicker than she would've imagined. Spitting out the regulator, she drew in sweet breaths of the warm, tropical night air.

Aiden surfaced next to her and put a finger to her lips, as if warning her to be silent. She tried to tread water but kicked the bottom and stood in chest deep water. Looking around, she saw a lot of leafy foliage that the moon barely penetrated and realized a slow current was going around her. She also noticed there was no salt taste in her mouth. Had they gone up a river?

He eased in next to her and whispered, "The tanks are out of oxygen. We'll leave them." He took her tank off and then her mask. She stayed close by his side as he waded to the side of the river and hid her equipment under a leafy overhang before doing the same with his own. Was he worried someone would find the equipment and know where they'd gone?

The river seemed quiet and deserted, with only occasional bird calls. Had they lost their pursuers? She could only pray they had. She shivered, remembering the sound of those bullets and the request that she give herself up. Aiden was a genius to get her out of the villa in time to avoid those men and then to think of using the scuba gear to escape. Had he known where the river was because the water was cooler or he'd sensed a current? She shivered again.

Aiden strapped his rucksack back on and took her hand again, tugging her into the deeper water. "The river is pretty shallow," he whispered, "but I'm going to swim us upstream until we hit something we can't get across. I need you to hold on to the straps of my bag, down low so my arms are free."

She nodded. He was her hero and her Aquaman. If anybody could keep her safe, it was Aiden.

She wrapped her palms around the straps of his bag, down by his hips. He plunged under the water again and within moments was propelling them upstream. Melene kept trying to kick to help out, but her legs were exhausted. She kept her head above water while Aiden took even, regular breaths every three strokes. His style, endurance, and strength were more impressive to her than ever.

They made fast progress up the river. She tried to keep her head low to minimize the drag and make it easier on Aiden, but she constantly listened for anything out of the ordinary. Shafts of moonlight lit up the river and the banks on both sides. They passed what looked like a zipline park, the lines going over and into the water. They passed a few roads, and she even saw the lights from some houses in the bushes at times.

From the bulrushes on the side of the river, she saw two red glowing orbs. She blinked to clear her vision. She must be going insane. What would be dark red and glowing and ... slowly gliding across the water toward her?

The shape got more defined and the glows brighter, and her stomach threatened to claw its way out of her throat. The glows were reflected moonlight in something's eyes, and unless she was hallucinating, the ugly, bumpy head of a crocodile was coming straight at them.

"Aiden," she screamed, yanking at his bag. She scrambled away from the crocodile and over Aiden's back.

He was pushed deeper into the water for a moment, then burst up. "What?"

"Crocodile," she cried out, forgetting to be quiet in her horror.

The river was only up to Aiden's neck at this spot, but she couldn't touch. Melene splashed backwards away from the creature as Aiden whipped out his pistol. She thought he was going to shoot the beast, but he didn't. She wanted to get out of this river right now, but she watched in frozen panic as the crocodile sliced right up to Aiden and opened his jaws wide.

Melene screamed. Aiden shot his pistol right into the beast's cavernous, horrifying mouth and the beast reared back. Aiden flung himself to the side and brought the butt of his pistol down right into one of those glowing red eyes. The glow disappeared. The crocodile made the most terrifying growling sound Melene had ever heard. It was a loud, deep-toned roar that seemed to reverberate from inside the creature and pulse through the air and the water.

Melene bit down on her own scream. If anyone was indeed following them, she'd probably alerted them to their location, or the gunshot had. Who cared who was following them when a crocodile was going to rip them apart?

The crocodile thrashed at Aiden, hitting into him from the side with that awful jaw and pointed, nasty teeth. Aiden aimed the gun into that cavernous pit of death and pulled the trigger again.

The crocodile let out another awful roar and then flung itself to the side and sank into the water. Had he finally killed it?

Aiden quickly swam to her and tugged her toward the opposite bank. "Time to get out of the water," he murmured in what sounded like an almost-teasing tone.

Melene's eyes were wide, and her entire body trembled. Were

there more crocodiles? Probably. Her eyes darted around as they swam for the bank and then waded onto it. Aiden stowed his flippers under some brush and then took her hand and walked at a quick pace along a semi-broken trail. Rocks and twigs poked at her feet, but she said nothing. Desperation and fear drove her on, but Aiden somehow steadied and comforted her. She could hardly believe he'd beaten a crocodile without breaking a sweat. He was some kind of superhero, maybe even more than Aquaman.

The river had been quietly running downstream, but the rushing of water became pronounced the farther up they went. Melene's legs were exhausted, and she couldn't stop shaking. She clung to Aiden's hand, her only source of comfort and sanity at this point, and just kept putting one foot in front of the other.

The rushing water grew louder. Her eyes had adjusted to the dim light and she could make out a waterfall above them. It was a different waterfall than she'd ever seen, with lots of boulders and pools interspersed up the gradual falls. It looked as if it had been landscaped and as if you could climb right up it.

"Let's go up it in case someone finds and tracks our footprints, or they bring dogs," Aiden instructed.

Dogs? Tracking footprints? Melene's heart raced. Her gaze darted around, but she saw nothing.

She had never climbed a waterfall, but she followed Aiden's path and he assisted her often. She was amazed that it wasn't too hard, and the rocks weren't slick. They made it up the waterfall, and the water was waist deep in the river above it. Aiden kept going through the river, not exiting it. She looked around desperately for more crocodiles and noticed Aiden's head swiveling as well. It was better on her feet to go through the river with its smooth rocks, but it was more tiring and nerve-wracking.

When she thought she couldn't move one more inch, Aiden finally guided her to the bank and they climbed out of the water. He directed her a short distance through thick trees and undergrowth and into a small clearing. He sat next to a large tree and rested his back against it, tugging her down next to him.

Melene all but collapsed, leaning against the tree.

"You okay?" he asked softly.

She tried to nod, hoping it looked convincing and hoping he couldn't see the fear and exhaustion in her eyes because of the semi-darkness surrounding them.

Aiden took his pack off and sorted through it. He pulled out his phone first and sent off a lengthy text. Apparently, he still worried someone would hear them because he wasn't speaking. If no one had heard the crocodile event, she assumed they were pretty safe. But she'd assumed they were safe talking to those boys and look where that had gotten them.

She was thirsty and hungry and scared and exhausted, but she was also so grateful. They'd escaped from a bunch of thugs with machine guns and from a crocodile. She was grateful to and for Aiden, and grateful to heaven above.

Aiden pulled a thick black water bottle out of his pack. He set the pack to the side, stood, and walked back to the river's edge. Unscrewing the lid, he filled the bottle and then screwed the lid back on as he walked back to her.

He settled down next to her and flipped the water bottle's lid open. "The straw is a filter," he said. "You thirsty? It's safe."

"Yes." She wrapped her lips around the straw and sucked in

the water. It wasn't cold, and she didn't care how clean or dirty it was. It tasted wonderful. She sucked down several long drinks, then handed it back to Aiden. He drank his fill and then went and refilled it.

He pulled some protein bars out of the pack and handed her one. She ate it quickly and then drank some more water. Resting back against the tree, her wet clothes clung to her and her teeth started chattering. It wasn't actually cold outside, but she was wet and chilled and the fear of what they'd been through and what still might be coming made her even more chilled.

Aiden wrapped his arms around her and drew her close. "Cold?" he murmured against her forehead, rubbing his hands up and down her arms.

"I don't know if it's cold or terror," she admitted.

He gently kissed her forehead. "You've done amazing, Melene. You're brave and you don't know the meaning of complaining. I'm so impressed with you."

"Thank you." She wanted to gush a row of compliments but settled for, "I think you're even tougher and cooler and more handsome than Aquaman."

He chuckled softly and kept rubbing her arms to get her warm. "You'd warm up faster with less clothes."

Her entire body felt a burst of warmth. "Don't you dare ask me to take my shirt off," she shot at him.

Aiden laughed. He easily lifted her onto his lap and then surrounded her with his broad chest and arms. "I wouldn't dream of asking that."

Melene never wanted him to let her go. She was still cold, wet, and tired, but at least she wasn't thirsty or as hungry. She realized as he held her that she wasn't terrified. At least not at the moment.

"Can we pray?" she asked.

"I would love that. Will you?"

She nodded against him, closed her eyes, and prayed, "Dear Father, thank you for protecting us, thank you for Aiden, thank you for guardian angels, thank you for life. Please keep us in thy watchful care. We love you. Amen."

Aiden echoed her amen, but then he released his grip on her. She instantly felt the loss. She was still on his lap and leaning against him. He pulled his bag closer and fished around for a few seconds, then pulled out a small plastic square. Ripping it open, he unfolded it and it became a plastic blanket. She recognized the emergency blankets that she usually had in her backpack for situations like this. Aiden tucked it around her and then wrapped his arms around the outside of the blanket to secure it tighter to her.

She burrowed into his firm chest, sliding her hands along the sides of his abdomen and glorying in the strength, warmth, and wonder of this man. He hadn't wanted her to get too invested; she hadn't wanted herself to get too invested. But it was far, far too late for that.

She loved him. Heart, body, and soul. She adored her Aquaman. They might die tonight and they might never escape the reaches of General Phillip.

She should ask him what the plan was. Try to keep her heart detached. She should do a lot of things. Instead, she looked up at him. It was still dark, but she was close enough she could see the depth in his blue eyes.

Then she kissed him.

Like earlier tonight, Aiden responded quickly and wholeheartedly. He seemed to pour himself into the kiss as he cradled her close. Aiden was a loyal and incredible man. She didn't believe he'd kiss her like this unless he felt as deeply for her as she did for him.

The kisses took on a life of their own, but suddenly Aiden pulled back and ushered her head into the crook of his neck. "Try to rest," he said in a husky, breathless tone.

Rest? She'd never wanted rest less than she did right now.

His heart was thundering against her chest and his breathing was irregular, just like hers. Melene instantly realized that he'd stopped the kissing to keep them under control. It was smart and rational, but she hated stopping. She wanted to trail kisses up his neck, across his jawline, and then capture his lips again.

Forcing herself to close her eyes, she begged for heavenly help for the hundredth time tonight. Here she went, asking far too much of her guardian angels again. This time she wasn't in danger from outside forces, but from her own desires. She'd stayed virtuous her entire life, and she didn't want to mess that up.

Suddenly, she had to know, though. She glanced up at Aiden and could see his jaw was clamped tight and his gaze was on her.

"Have you ever been intimate?" she asked him in a rush, heat filling her face.

Aiden blinked down at her. His jaw softened and his gaze was full of her. "No."

She stared at him. "That's impressive."

"Thank you." His gaze became penetrating. "What about you?"

She shook her head. "I'm saving myself for marriage." Her

doubts and fears of the future swirled around her. "If I ever do get married."

He only stared at her, as if he had no clue how to respond to that. Finally, he said, "Can you rest?"

She probably couldn't and she'd prefer talking to him or kissing a lot more, but she leaned her cheek against the smooth muscle of his shoulder and closed her eyes.

Marriage. Would that ever happen for her or for Aiden? Most likely, the answer was no. And that shouldn't scare her as much as everything else they'd faced tonight.

Chapter Twelve

Aiden stared around at the clearing, listening to any nuance in sound and trying to avoid staring at Melene's gorgeous face. It was hard enough to stay in control with her firm body cradled in his arms and the memory of their intense kisses in his mind.

She'd finally settled in against him, her breathing had evened out, and she'd fallen asleep. That helped cool his ardor a bit.

Saving myself for marriage. If I ever do get married.

Those two lines were on repeat in his brain. He'd tried to stop himself from becoming enraptured with her, but it was far, far too late for that. If only he could be the man she'd saved herself for. If only they could get married and have their own happily ever after. He grimaced. They had to make it through tonight first, and they had to keep her safe from Phillip and get that bounty removed.

If all of that worked out, would he dare ask her if they could make some kind of long-distance relationship work? With both of their jobs and travel, they'd most likely be on different continents at all times. Creating a relationship between them was idealistically naïve and doomed to failure. He couldn't stand the thought of letting her go, but the thought of marriage and children and him either being killed or Melene growing to resent him being gone and in danger all the time scared him. He knew they were different than Jace and Charisse but he could almost see them ending up in a worst spot.

Dawn was fast approaching, and he wondered how long he had until someone approached and they had to move, or he got the signal from Thor and Greer to move to a more open location where the chopper could extract them. Papa had immediately changed the plan when he'd gotten Aiden's text. Instead of flying directly to Jamaica, Thor and Greer had rerouted to the nearby Guantanamo Bay Military Base in Cuba. A Black Hawk helicopter with only the pilot, Thor, and Greer onboard, would fly to Jamaica to retrieve them and then take them on to an undetermined location. Aiden imagined Papa knew their next stop was, but he wasn't about to text it and risk any interception, even with secure phones.

His phone beeped in his pocket. He tried not to disturb Melene as he retrieved it, but she woke and slid off his lap. He hated the loss of her close, but it would make it easier for him to think clearly.

"Everything okay?" she asked.

He nodded and pulled his phone out. Thor had texted coordinates as close as he could find to where Aiden was. He clicked on them and his phone immediately showed the map. Zero point four miles away. He groaned. It was close, but without shoes, it would not be easy.

"We've got a bit of a walk," he admitted to Melene.

As he was coming to realize was her innate and impressive good nature, she simply nodded, stood, and stretched. Aiden tried not to stare. Her tank top and shorts were still damp and clung to her. He pulled his knife out, pulled a roll of gauze out of his bag's medical kit, and then cut the plastic blanket up. He fished out a small roll of duct tape from a pocket.

"Sit and give me a foot," he instructed Melene.

She smiled questioningly, but obeyed. He wrapped the gauze and then some of the plastic around her foot and duct-taped them on, repeating the process on her other foot.

"You're incredible," she gushed, giving him a quick hug and a kiss on the lips.

Aiden grinned, wishing he could extend the hug and kiss. Maybe when they got to their next location. With Thor and Greer watching on. That might be awkward to have his brothers as their audience but he didn't care. Those two had found the loves of their lives. They could handle watching him hold Melene night and day.

He grimaced. He was the one who couldn't handle that and stay in control. If they weren't running for their lives, he'd beg her to elope. He shook his head at himself. There was no future for him and this beauty. Neither of them would change their calling in life. He had to stop letting himself be deluded into imagining there was a way to navigate a relationship.

Melene eased back with a questioning look when he didn't respond. He quickly wrapped his own feet, secured the gauze and plastic with duct tape, and stored everything back in the bag. He offered Melene a drink, took a drink himself, and refilled his water bottle from the stream. They were headed away from the river to a clearing. He didn't know if they'd found a spot they could land the helicopter or just drop a line.

Shrugging his tactical backpack on, he led the way. He and Melene trudged through the thick foliage. It was rough going and he wished for a machete. His pocketknife wasn't cutting it and he didn't dare push down trees and make too much noise. At least the foot protection was a little better than bare feet. He stepped on a sharp rock and hid a wince. A little better.

He heard some movement in the brush to their right. Freezing, he tugged Melene behind him, drew his gun out, and scanned the area for the source of the noise. He was concerned, but only because of Melene's safety. He would happily go back and fight all those men who had invaded their sanctuary last night. Maybe he'd get his chance right now.

Melene's panting breaths at his back were almost as loud as whatever was pushing through the brush. The movement kept coming, but no head or body. He looked down and could see a pig snuffling through the brush, and then the animal snorted indignantly at them before pushing past.

He turned to Melene. "Just a pig."

She gave him a trembling smile. He could see she was almost at the end of her rope. If only he could gather her into his arms and comfort her. Now wasn't the time.

Would it ever be "the time" for them?

He hated to give her false hope that they could be together when he couldn't see a clear path to go forward. One minute he wanted to hang all the future issues and just kiss her until she knew how much he cared and how incredible she was. The next, he knew he had to keep his distance so he didn't hurt her. It felt like his emotions were on a roller coaster ride and he honestly had no clue how to respond, as he'd never been here before.

He squeezed her hand and then started walking again. Keeping her safe had to be the priority right now. He lost his mind when she kissed him. If she leaned in again, he'd have to turn his head. That would suck.

They walked through more jungle and finally reached the extraction site. It was a large area that had been cleared of trees, probably centuries ago, and planted into sugar cane. He thought the area they were closest to may have been where the old plantation home and outbuildings had been. He'd heard about slave rebellions years ago where the plantation owners were murdered and the houses and outbuildings burned to the ground. Squinting, he could see some foundations through the murky light. It looked to be a decent-sized house.

Interesting. These people lived and died and some died violently while others' lives improved because of those deaths and they lived to carry on. All that was left of the struggle and their lives was some stone. What would be left when Aiden died? His family would definitely mourn him, and his teammates, but what had he built? What legacy did he have?

He shook off the odd thoughts and focused on the mission as he always did. Melene was safe, and there was room for a chopper to land here.

He stopped and turned to her. "This is the spot. Here's hoping Thor and Greer aren't too far out."

She smiled wanly. "I'll pray for that."

He studied her, wanting to tell her how incredible she was, but then he heard the low thrum of chopper blades. That was good. He turned and looked into the predawn sky. He could see some lights coming their way. He was excited to see his brothers and get off his feet, and eating some decent food after his long swim would be great.

Any minute now and he and Melene would be safe, headed for a safe location, and he'd have help to protect her. He loved being her hero and being alone with her, but he was used to being part of a team. His flesh and blood brothers were every bit as qualified, tough, and reliable as his SEAL brothers. Maybe he could relax a little ... and kiss Melene. That wasn't the smartest, or most rational, plan he'd ever had, but it sure was the most exciting one.

He risked a glance at her. She was looking up at the sky as well, but she dropped her gaze to his and an enchanting smile blossomed on her face. He couldn't stop his body from swaying closer to her, as if he'd already given himself permission to kiss away. Her dark eyes beaconed him closer and he knew resistance was futile.

Another sound had him yanking away from Melene and pivoting toward the west. Lights were coming up the road, a truck rumbling straight for their location. He didn't know if whoever was in that truck was a danger to Melene, but he was taking no chances after two innocent boys may have unknowingly caused the past seven hours of stress. He wrapped his arm around her and ushered her back to the coverage of the trees.

She trembled against him.

"It's okay," he whispered against her hairline. "Probably nothing to do with us. They're probably workers coming to work in the sugar cane fields before it gets too hot." It wasn't yet five a.m. and the Jamaicans had a reputation for being laid-back. It worried him that this truck might not be any workers but someone who was looking for them.

If the men who'd attacked the villa figured out they'd swam away in the ocean, they would probably guess he'd take one of the river tributaries up into the mountains. It made him ponder if a worker at the resort had actually put the pieces together and not the little boys. Someone could've been watching them at their pool or their beach and gotten a picture. Maybe a resort security camera had gotten an angle on Melene's face and a guard had figured out who she was. That actually made more sense as those men had come at the villa with guns a-blazing only two hours after the interaction with the little boys. Also, they'd known Melene's name. He and his team would've snuck in and incapacitated their target, but obviously those mercenaries didn't know the meaning of subtlety.

What other options were there for their discovery? He might never know. The little boys may have saved their lives, as he'd been packed and ready to go the moment they needed to escape.

He pushed the unanswered questions away. The focus of the moment was the truck stopping next to the fields and the handful of men spilling out. Thankfully, Aiden had backup. The chopper was coming in hot.

The men started screaming and waving off the olive-green military chopper. They didn't pull any weapons out, so that calmed him a fraction, but they may have just been waiting to see who they were dealing with before they revealed their firepower.

The Blackhawk descended and touched down. The doors opened and Thor and Greer leaped out. They each held an M240 machine gun like they meant business, pointed straight at the men in the truck.

The men scrambled back into the truck, pushing, screeching, and elbowing each other to get there first. The driver popped it into gear and the older truck was spinning around and flying back down the road before the passenger door was shut.

Aiden laughed out loud. Man, he loved his brothers, and that timing had been perfect.

Who knew if those men were dangerous to Melene, or simply unfortunate workers who were crapping down both legs right now? Aiden was just relieved they'd bugged out so easily.

He kept his arm around Melene and ushered her back out into the clearing.

Both Thor and Greer turned as they sensed the motion. Aiden hurried into the circle of light from the chopper so they could see him. The wind created by the chopper's blades whipped Melene's hair around her face and sent stinging dirt at their faces and any exposed skin.

His brothers both immediately lowered their weapons. Thor's face broke into a huge grin, and he hurried toward them. Greer's smile was a lot slower and more reluctant, but Aiden could see their next younger brother was ecstatic and relieved. Greer never showed much emotion or talked more than a few words at a time. As kids, they'd teased him a lot and had rarely riled him. Then he reached six-five and the fact that he had the twins by a couple inches and was as muscular and fit as both of them meant they didn't tease as much, but they still wrestled and fought.

Thor reached him and slung his free arm around Aiden's neck, yelling, "Yes! There is the ugliest twin brother in the world."

"Good thing we're not identical or I'd have to wear a mask night and day. The world can only handle one face that looks that bad," Aiden hollered back.

"You mean the women can only handle one face this irresistibly handsome." Thor laughed. "Hi, Melene. Let's get you out of here."

Thor released him and gestured toward the chopper. Aiden hurried Melene through the artificial windstorm and lifted her into the cabin. He jumped in himself, extending his hand and pulling Thor, then Greer in, getting a backslap from Thor and a nod from Greer.

Greer slammed the door behind them. They all took seats and strapped in as the pilot lifted off. Aiden tugged on the headset and the rest of them did the same.

Aiden wanted to reach for Melene's hand. He wasn't sure if it was to reassure her or to reassure himself. He liked having her close. It comforted and strengthened him. And he couldn't remember ever needing either comfort or strength from anyone but heaven since he'd left home and his mama's endearing worries.

"Pilot is on this frequency too. Our friend Captain John. Great guy," Thor said in what sounded like a friendly, informative voice, but Aiden caught the meaning. Don't say Melene's name or anything else that we might not want to leak. Captain John is most likely the best of the best and wouldn't leak information if they pulled off his toenails, but just in case ...

"Thanks for coming for us, Captain John," Aiden said.

"My pleasure."

Thor was still grinning at him. "Man, it's great to see you. Does this mean you're bringing that ugly face to my wedding? I have a tux all lined up for you, but even dressing you up might not help much. Would it be offensive if your backside was to the crowd as the best man? Since we all know that's your only tolerable side to look at for any length of time."

Greer only shook his head at Thor, but the pilot gave a surprised chuckle and Melene smiled.

Aiden grinned. "Your poor bride. What is the wedding party going to do when the preacher says, 'You may kiss the bride' and Shelly begs, 'Please no. I have to look at that face the rest of my life. You expect me to kiss it too?'"

Thor guffawed, Melene laughed, the pilot laughed, and even Greer let out a small chuckle.

"You two," Melene said. "I'd forgotten how you're always teasing each other."

"It's not teasing," Thor protested. "They really do ask me to keep the ugly twin overseas to keep our family stock prices up. We've even snuck in some family pictures of the rest of the gorgeous crew that he hasn't been able to ruin."

They went back and forth arguing about who was the most handsome, or the most ugly, taking jabs at each other, and laughing a lot. Even the pilot and Greer threw in a few comments.

Aiden relaxed into the seat, relishing that they were safe and that his brothers were here. He ached to reach for Melene's hand, but when he glanced at her, he realized she'd fallen asleep.

Thor's gaze went in her direction. "Rough night?" he asked softly.

"Pretty crazy," Aiden said, which was saying something as he'd had many crazier nights with the SEALs, but he hadn't had a beautiful sweetheart that he cared too deeply for in his protection those nights.

"Well, you look like crap warmed over, so you probably should try to sleep a bit too," Thor said.

"I met a crocodile tonight who was better looking than you, and that's nothing beauty sleep can fix," Aiden threw back at him. He was still smiling, but the thought of that croc almost hurting Melene made a chill go down his spine.

Thor chuckled. "That sounds like a story I need to hear."

Aiden proceeded to tell them the story. The other three men were shocked that the first shot point blank in the mouth hadn't killed the beast. They kept chatting and swapping stories about hunting, fishing, crocodiles, and other tales that were probably embellished, especially if Thor was telling them.

Aiden should've slept, but he enjoyed this time with his brothers far too much. Man, he'd missed them both. He missed all of his family, but being absentee from home most of the time was the life he'd chosen. For this moment, he was happy and Melene was safe.

If only he could take Melene's hand. Or better yet, hold her. Holding her would give him the sense of home and comfort he hadn't known he was missing until he'd started protecting her. Did he have the faith to push past the fear of an unknown future and beg Melene to do the same?

He focused on his brothers and the teasing chatter. No matter how brave he thought he was, he didn't know how to overcome his relationship fears.

Chapter Thirteen

Melene woke to daylight, someone touching her arm, and the loud sound of ... she looked around and realized it was a helicopter. It all came rushing back. Hers and Aiden's crazy swim of escape, complete with a crocodile attack. It would've been the stuff of nightmares if Aiden hadn't been there. Then his brothers had come for them. Were they finally safe?

The helicopter blades shut down, and she heard the pilot talking with Thor about refueling and heading back.

"Good morning, sunshine," Aiden said.

She blinked and stretched, her neck kinked from the awkward sleeping position. "Hi," she managed, suddenly shy and wondering how awful she looked with frizzy hair, disheveled clothes, and no makeup. She hadn't thought about money since Aiden told her Papa would be offended if she tried to repay him, but now they were moving to a new location and Thor and Greer were involved. She usually was the one giving charity, not receiving it. This experience was helping her understand the people who refused help or were embarrassed by it. The uncertainty of not knowing if she'd have clean clothes and a toothbrush bothered her, but having to beg someone for either bothered her more.

They were safe for the moment. She'd focus on that.

The sun was bright and high overhead as Aiden helped her out of the helicopter. The men thanked the pilot. Aiden smiled at her in concern as he escorted her to a Land Rover parked behind a huge airplane hangar. She glanced around. She couldn't see much past a few more corrugated-sided airplane hangars, a couple small airplanes, and a lot of trees.

Aiden helped her into the backseat of the vehicle behind the driver and hurried around, climbing in opposite her and slinging his bag into the back. Thor and Greer handed over three duffel bags to Aiden and then climbed up front while he tossed theirs into the back as well. Would Aiden have asked Papa Delta to have clothes and toiletries waiting for her at this new location?

Greer drove. They motored quickly through a quiet, private airport and then along some tree-lined streets. She could see lush mountains towering so high the tops were lost to the clouds. "Where are we?" she asked when no one spoke. The men must be tired. She remembered falling asleep to their hilarious and nonstop banter. Was she the only one who'd slept?

"La Fortuna, Costa Rica," Thor informed her. He turned slightly in his seat. "Now we couldn't pry info out of you while our buddy John was listening in, but it's just us trustworthy Delta men now." His look was concerned. "How are you holding up, Melene?" His blue eyes glinted with mischief. "And how on earth have you survived days alone with that horrifying face next to you?"

Melene laughed, relaxing. She loved the Delta family. It wouldn't be awkward with Thor and Greer here, though she'd miss time alone with Aiden.

"I'm great, Thor. Thank you for coming for me. Especially so close to your wedding. You too, Greer. I can never thank you all enough."

Greer nodded in acknowledgment.

"It's okay that he doesn't talk. He's emotionally stunted," Thor explained, grinning at his younger but taller brother. "I'll take his thanks for him. The only pretty lady he talks for is his girl-friend Emery."

"Greer, you have a *girlfriend*?" Melene didn't mean to put so much shock into her voice. Greer was incredibly handsome like all the Delta men, but he was so painfully quiet she couldn't imagine how he'd meet or get to know a woman.

He only grunted, but Thor and Aiden laughed uproariously at her comment.

"I know, it's hard to believe," Thor said. "But Emery is gone over her strong, silent cowboy. Thankfully, the rest of the Delta men look like me, not Aiden." Thor's voice was teasing, but his eyes glinted happily. He was obviously thrilled his brother had found the right woman for him.

"That's wonderful. I'm sure she's amazing," Melene said.

"She's an angel," Greer said.

Her eyebrows went up and she couldn't resist exchanging a look with Aiden. He grinned conspiratorially at her, then reached over and took her hand. She relished the warm pressure of his hand, feeling settled and at home. She hoped the simple move meant he wouldn't keep his distance from her now his brothers were here. He'd definitely get teased for anything he did, at least from Thor.

"Word is the beautiful Emery has Greer chattering like a monkey," Aiden confided to Melene.

"Yep," Greer drawled, focusing on the road as they turned up a steeper but still paved road with thick trees encroaching on the sport utility.

Thor glanced back at them to say something, but he noticed their joined hands and his eyebrows popped up. "Well ... okay, then. Is *that* how it's going to be?" His gaze darted between them with a challenge and a mischievous glint.

"Yep," Melene drawled out, trying to imitate Greer and squeezing Aiden's hand.

Thor busted up at that. "Well, all right. We'll take over this security detail and try to give you two some space, then." He winked.

Melene flushed. She glanced at Aiden. He was giving her a warm look, and hope fluttered in her chest. Would they have more time to talk and kiss at this new sanctuary with his brothers watching over them? She should worry about the future and them going their separate ways, but at this point she doubted General Phillip was going to give up on his quest to flush her out with bribes and pictures or whatever he was doing. She wanted to enjoy Aiden. How long would these men sacrifice their time to keep her safe? Also, why did it seem like Thor and Greer had military training? They'd come out of that helicopter with huge weapons as if they were Rambo reincarnated. She didn't know how to ask that without offending them. All the Deltas were tough, and she imagined being ranchers, they had to know how to handle a gun to protect their livestock.

"What about your wedding?" she asked Thor. "Will you need to postpone it because you're helping me?"

Thor gave her a charming grin, his blue eyes twinkling. It was hilarious how he and Aiden teased each other about being ugly when they were both off-the-charts handsome. Especially Aiden.

"That's mighty kind of you to worry, Melene, but are you even looking at all of this?" He gestured to himself. "Shelly would 'wait at the altar for years for her handsome, charming, irresistible cowboy'. That's a direct quote."

Aiden burst out in laughter, Melene joined him, and even Greer guffawed.

"Don't believe him," Aiden told her. "He exaggerates everything. Thor worked for years, groveling and acting like a simp lord to convince Shelly to marry him. He'd never stop crying if the wedding didn't happen."

"Not true," Thor protested. "First of all, you call me a simp again and you'll find yourself outside this Land Rover, running to catch up. Second of all, she was pining over me for all those years."

"First of all, you'd be the one eating dust, but I'd love to see you attempt it for the thousandth time," Aiden shot back. "And second of all ... Greer, tell Melene the truth about Shelly and Thor," Aiden appealed to his quiet brother.

"Aiden's right," Greer reaffirmed. "Thor's a simp."

Aiden crowed in victory while Thor slugged Greer hard in the shoulder. Greer didn't even react, and the vehicle didn't so much as swerve.

Melene laughed at their nonstop banter. She suddenly missed her two younger sisters fiercely. They teased differently than boys, and were much nicer, but the underlying love and connection were the same.

They turned off the road into a steep driveway. Seconds later, Greer pulled to a stop, jumped out, hurried to a garage door, and flipped up a keypad. A pair of two-car garage doors seemed to comprise the basement level of a towering, four-story house. Melene looked up at the glistening white stucco and glass house. It was massive, and it looked light and airy like it was floating into the greenery and part of the clouds. She could hardly wait to explore it and hoped she wasn't putting a huge dent in the Delta family finances. How could she bring that up again?

Glancing around, she could only see thick trees and towering mountain slopes. She prayed no one would see them or find them here.

The garage door slid up and Greer returned, drove the vehicle in, and parked it. Melene opened her door and climbed out, stretching.

"Greer, your big brothers trained you better than that," Thor called. "Why didn't you open the lady's door?"

Greer hadn't left the driver's seat. He slid out and held up his phone by way of explanation to why he hadn't moved quick enough to avoid Thor calling him out because Melene was seated right behind him. Melene could see the name Emery at the top and a picture of a gorgeous, smiling lady with long, dark curly hair.

"Sorry," Greer grunted.

"I can open my own door," Melene told him. She leaned closer. "May I?"

Greer gave her the biggest smile she'd ever seen on his face, clicked on the picture, and zoomed in. Melene could see the happy radiance in the woman's smile and dark eyes.

"Wow, she is a beautiful angel," she told Greer.

"I'm blessed," Greer said.

"I'm sure she feels the same."

Greer ducked his head slightly, but he was still smiling.

Thor and Aiden walked to them, hauling the bags.

"Emery is so gone over him it hurts to watch," Thor told her, smiling happily. "Of course, not as gone as Shelly is over me. That's no surprise as Greer isn't capable of more than grunts or occasional 'yeps'. Who knows how pathetic his kissing is when he can't even talk?"

Greer moved so quick Melene hardly saw him coming. Grabbing Thor in a headlock, Greer punched him hard in the gut. Thor tossed the bags in his hand and elbowed him in the jaw.

She jumped back out of the way. Aiden dropped his bag and wrapped his arm around her. She felt settled and safe and happy.

Greer and Thor were trading punches and wrestling on the garage floor as Thor kept talking and taunting and Greer grunted and even laughed.

"Come on." Aiden ushered her toward the entry into the house. "They'll be at it for a minute. Perimeter check and security sensors and cameras set up, please," Aiden said to his brothers as they battled it out. "I'll do the interior check."

She looked back as Aiden swung the door to reveal stairs leading up. Thor's head seemed bent at an unnatural level, and he was still smiling. "You got it, bro," Thor called to them. "I'll only be a minute."

"Is he okay?" she asked.

"He's in heaven. The only thing he likes better than fighting is kissing Shelly."

"That's right, bro," Thor called. "We'll be up as soon as I pummel our little brother into submission and set up the security."

Greer was a couple inches taller than Thor, but they were both fit and strong. It looked like an even match, but they would both get their share of bruises. Melene was grateful not to watch the fight.

"Boys," she muttered as she and Aiden climbed the stairs.

Aiden chuckled. "You and your sisters don't wrestle, punch, or insult each other for fun?"

"Heavens no." She was seven years older than her sister Jessica and twelve years older than Abigail. She adored her beautiful sisters and couldn't imagine punching either of them. "Can you imagine what Gramma Larue would do to me if I punched Abigail?"

"Good point. I love Mama Larue, but she's feisty."

Aiden pulled his gun out and led the way. She appreciated his caution. "Papa didn't have someone setup cameras and sensors here?" she asked.

"No one he trusted lived nearby," he said.

They walked through a clean laundry and mud room and then into a massive and beautiful open living area. There were windows and bright white everywhere. The only thing that wasn't white was the stainless-steel appliances in the kitchen and a pale blue and gray swirled granite countertop and gray-bricked fireplace. The home was gorgeous and modern, and the sun lit everything brightly with all the floor-to-ceiling two-story windows. The back windows overlooked a large pool and hot tub with the trees and the mountains framing the space.

"Wow. This is insane."

"Decent spot to hide out for a bit," Aiden said.

They strolled through the rest of the house, touring eight master suites on levels two and three, and a game room, a theater, a workout room, and a playroom on level four.

"If we survive, I'm going to beg my parents to rent this place for a family reunion," she told Aiden as they stood in the hallway of the fourth floor, the open stairway next to them that was open all the way down to the main level. Windows that ran four levels and a crazy long chandelier that dripped down the middle of the stairwell like a waterfall lit up the bright and unique staircase.

She winced at her own words. After she paid Papa Delta back for renting this place for her protection detail, she'd talk to her parents about a family reunion.

He blinked at her. "If we survive? You've got nothing to worry about, especially now that Thor and Greer are here to back me up."

She felt as if she'd insulted him. "I'm sorry. Of course I trust you to protect me. I just meant ..."

Aiden eased in closer, his blue eyes reassuring. "It's okay. I wasn't offended. I just want you to feel safe."

"I do, with you." She had no clue where she and Aiden stood or if there would ever be a future possible for them, but she couldn't resist throwing her arms around his neck and hugging him. "Thank you for being my Aquaman."

He grinned, and he dipped his head to kiss her.

Loud footsteps and Thor's carrying voice came up the stairs to them.

Aiden pulled back, and she tasted disappointment instead of his lips.

"This place is sweet," Thor was saying. "Do you think we'd dare jump off that third-floor deck to the pool?"

"No," Greer said shortly.

"Hey, you two," Thor called up. He was still a flight of stairs away, but must've seen them. "Don't worry, I beat Greer into submission and I've got the bags and I setup the security sensors and cameras and did a perimeter check." He hefted three bags while Greer carried one. "No, it's okay. I know I do all the work and I carry the bags all the time. I know you worry about me feeling like a mule, but I've got it." He reached them and handed Aiden's bag to him and then put a smaller duffel bag in Melene's hands.

Greer simply shook his head, not refuting that Thor had done all the work, though Melene highly doubted Greer hadn't helped or possibly done more than Thor.

"What's this?" Melene asked.

"Our incredible sister, Esther, got a text from your boyfriend here, so she packed you a bag of toiletries and clothes just in case you had to move quick and leave yours behind." He winked. "And look at that. You did. Thoughtful guy, my brother, even if he is ugly."

"Yes, he is. Thoughtful not ugly. Ultra-handsome actually."

Thor and Aiden both smiled.

Melene hugged the bag to her chest the way she longed to hug Aiden. "Tell Esther thank you."

"I will. Did you know she and Sheriff Reed fell in love?"

"I didn't." Melene smiled, imagining those two impressive people together. "I love that."

"We do too. Reed's a stud. Now." Thor clapped his hands together. "Do you want to shower, sleep, or eat first?"

"Shower," Melene said, though her stomach was grumbling.

Aiden nodded. "Choose any bedroom," he told her. "These two cowboys might seem incompetent, but they're actually both incredible cooks. They'll make us a late lunch."

"Incompetent," Thor muttered. "You'll regret that when I scrounge up some dog poop to add to your lunch."

Aiden smiled. "You wouldn't dare. I'd have Greer thump you again."

"Greer?" Thor exclaimed. "Thump me?" He put a hand to his chest.

Aiden looked to Greer. "You pinned him in the garage in less than a minute, didn't you? That's how you got the sensors and cameras set up so fast."

"Yep." Greer smiled.

Thor shouted in outrage. Melene laughed.

Aiden shook his head. "You'd better go choose a room and shower. He'll be arguing about who won and how he's going to 'thrash' us for hours. Maybe if you worked out as much as you yapped," Aiden said to his twin.

Melene smiled as Thor protested again. She lifted a hand to all the brothers, but her gaze was focused on Aiden. "Thanks." He was so thoughtful to arrange yet another set of clothes and toiletries.

"See you soon." Aiden did a manly lift of his chin, his blue eyes full of her.

She almost tripped walking away. She could feel Aiden's eyes on her back as Thor took up the arguing and the insults again. There was so much love in the brothers' teasing it made her homesick for her family and happy Aiden could be with his. It also made her miss all the children she worked with. The children didn't usually trade insults like the Delta twins, but they teased and laughed and always made her smile. She missed being the one taking care of others, but she had to admit Aiden taking care of her, being here for her, risking his life for her, holding her hand ... it all added up to a sense of home and happiness she hadn't realized she was longing for.

Walking down the stairs, she wondered where her place and her future was. She'd gotten so involved and busy the days just slid by and she didn't question her future plans, but Aiden was flipping everything upside down. Was she meant to be with the children serving them as she'd always assumed? Should she return to Summit Valley with her family where she would be safe and loved? Could she simply cling to her incredible Aquaman, one Aiden Delta? But he had important missions and the fear of something happening to him wasn't something she could push away.

She sighed. If only heaven would give her a neon sign. She had no clue where her place was and she didn't like the indecision and worry of her future, her safety, and putting these men out to protect her. None of them made her feel like that, but she worried. She needed to have faith that it would all work out like she and

Aiden had talked about when he'd showed her the scripture tattooed on his back.

The worries still lingered.

If...

If Thor truly had to reschedule his wedding, she'd feel awful.

If General Phillip found them, her life would be over.

If Aiden went back to the SEALs without a second glance after this was over, she'd be devastated.

Chapter Fourteen

Aiden took a long shower while Thor and Greer cooked for them. It was nice to let down his guard a bit. The shower enclosure had two walls of glass and overlooked the pool area below, the marble surround only covering the essentials on the window side. This house was insanely gorgeous and unique.

Melene was more insanely gorgeous and unique.

He rested his forehead against the glass wall and stared sightlessly at the view of mountains and trees.

He was so gone over Melene. What was he going to do when this was over and they had to go their separate ways? He'd never felt so torn up inside at the very thought of a person not being by his side every moment. He'd left his family behind to serve his country. It had been rough and had sometimes gouged at him, but he'd survived. He'd been separated from close friends in the military because of assignments. It had stunk, but he'd gotten through it. He'd lost comrades in arms and wished he could've died with them. It had been horrific.

Somehow, he thought nothing could be as hard as saying goodbye to Melene.

Finally shutting off the shower, he dressed in a T-shirt and hybrid shorts, brushed his teeth and hair, and splashed on some cologne. He hurried through the third story, listening but not hearing any movement in Melene's suite. There were four master bedrooms on each of the second and third floors. Thor had amazingly not teased him when Aiden took the suite next to Melene's and both his brothers had gratefully gone down a flight to take rooms on the second floor.

He pumped down the stairs, picking up a loud male voice and a sweet female voice on the main level. He burst onto the main level, his gaze immediately drawn to the dark-haired beauty chatting with Thor as his brothers finished up what looked to be a taco bar.

She was wearing a pretty floral top and fitted shorts—good job Esther on picking clothes. Her long, dark hair flowed down her back.

Melene turned to him with a beautiful smile. "Hi." It was such a simple word, but it seemed to have a mountain of possibilities. Hi, let's spend the rest of the day talking and kissing. Hi, I'm falling in love with you. Hi, let's spend the rest of eternity together.

The fear of eternity never working out for them pressed in, but he shoved it away as hard as he would Thor coming at him.

"Hey," he managed, hurrying to her side.

"All the pretty cologne in the world can't make up for that

ugly mug," Thor teased him as Aiden approached. "Did you think if you showered long enough, it could remedy that face?"

Aiden chuckled and dipped a chip into the homemade guacamole, plunging it into his mouth. It was fabulous, a little salt, lime, garlic, jalapeno, and cilantro blended with the savory avocado. He hadn't been lying about his brothers' cooking abilities.

"Maybe you could try a shower so we didn't have to smell or look at your disgustingness for a few minutes."

"Oh-ho! Maybe if my bossy big brother didn't demand I cook for him."

Aiden was only a few minutes older than Thor and usually he was the one who brought it up.

"Since I am the oldest, I have the authority."

They all laughed and teased as they dished up plates with homemade tortillas, seasoned steak and chicken cooked in thin strips with onions, peppers, and mushrooms, cilantro lime rice, black beans, creamy street corn, and topped it all off with lettuce, tomato, cheese, sour cream, homemade *pico de galo*, and the fabulous guacamole. Aiden could hardly get his mouth around his first bite. It was bursting with flavor and welcome manna after the night they had last night and not eating anything besides a couple of protein bars.

They swapped stories about everything that had happened since Aiden first rescued Melene from General Phillip. Then Melene drew out the story of how Thor broke through Shelly's walls and got engaged. That story gave Aiden plenty of opportunity to throw jabs at his twin, but he also loved seeing how Thor glowed as he talked about his rodeo queen, the "fastest and most beautiful barrel-racer in the country". He was desperately in love with Shelly and it made Aiden very happy.

He risked a glance at Melene. How would it be to know they were both going to settle down in Summit Valley, have children together in a home full of love, build a legacy that wouldn't crumble like those stones at the plantation in Jamaica?

He pushed that away and focused on the conversation as they ate until they were stuffed, then cleaned up lunch and went to lounge by the gorgeous pool. Usually Aiden hated sitting around, but he was exhausted from not sleeping and going so hard last night and all he wanted was to listen to Melene talk and stare at her beautiful face.

The pool area was even prettier than the one in Jamaica, minus the ocean. Aiden didn't like being away from the ocean. Apparently, La Fortuna was in the "cloud forest" of Costa Rica and several hours from the closest beach. He'd survive for a few days without being in the ocean. His family had never understood why he needed the ocean and not the mountains like their home in Colorado. He'd spent many hours in the lake, but it was freezing cold and inaccessible in the winter. Nothing was like the ocean for Aiden. He stared at Melene as she laughed at something Thor had said. Nothing but Melene.

Melene impressively drew out the story from Greer, with Thor adding in juicy and sometimes false details, about how Greer and Emery fell in love. It was a pretty insane story as Greer had shot and killed Emery's only brother Travis to save the lives of their cousin Alivia and her now-fiancé Klein. Emery had been tricked by the very man who sent Travis to steal the Delta family secret. She had gone to Greer to avenge her brother's death. Of course Greer and Thor both omitted any reference to the secret, simply saying Alivia and Klein had been kidnapped.

The story was long and detailed, especially for Greer, and it was incredible to see how in love Greer was with Emery. It made Aiden incredibly happy. And it carried a sting of jealousy and guilt for him. No matter how he wanted to make it work in his head, he and Melene would never have a happily ever after like his brothers and older sister could now claim.

As the conversation settled, Thor decided it was time to swim. Melene went and put a suit on and Aiden couldn't drag his gaze from her in a white floral two-piece that contrasted beautifully with her smooth brown skin. He would give his sister a big hug and thank you when he saw Esther again.

He and his brothers took turns climbing anything they could find from a stone wall to the third-story balcony that Greer had been uncertain was a smart move. They tucked their legs up and didn't hit the bottom of the pool too hard. They also covered Melene with water from their cannonballs. She cautioned them to be careful until Thor started calling her "Mom," then she switched to rating their cannonballs, flips, or dives from a nearby lounge chair.

The afternoon wore into evening as they played as only brothers could do, Melene's presence making everything sparkle and more fun. Aiden noticed his brothers' occasional surveillance of their surroundings and they all listened for any beep from their phones, but all was quiet. It was nice to let down his guard, knowing Thor and Greer were here to help.

Sunset came really early with the tall mountains surrounding them. It wasn't dark, but dim, and the mountains and a low fog made it ethereal and romantic. Aiden wondered if he'd ever thought a setting was romantic before. With Melene around, he couldn't stop those thoughts. He propelled himself out of the pool, walked to her lounge chair, scooped her into his arms, and smiled at her little cry of surprise.

"It's time for you to swim, not just judge our performance," he told her.

Melene smiled. "I'd say I don't want to wash my hair again, but you three have soaked me so many times that argument is a little lame."

She slid her arms around his neck and leaned into him. Aiden's heart sped triple time.

"I wouldn't listen to it anyway," he told her. He noticed his brothers were strangely silent in the pool. They'd been taking turns seeing who could swim more lengths of it. Of course he'd blown past anything they could do, and he hadn't even been trying that hard. Put him on a horse and these two could desecrate him, but water was his home.

She gave a mock cry of outrage. "I'll have you know a woman's hair is extremely important."

He walked to the side of the pool, holding her tightly against him, the warm skin of her legs and abdomen under his palms making his thoughts scatter. "You don't seem the type to waste much time worrying about your hair."

She glanced coyly up at him. "Only when you're around to impress."

He grinned. "I'm impressed."

She returned his smile.

He jumped to the side, and she clung tighter to him and

gasped as they plunged into the warm water of the deep end. They surfaced and water glistened off her beautiful face. He treaded water with only his legs, refusing to relinquish his hold on her now that he had her exactly where he wanted her.

"I think that's our cue to go shower our handsome selves and cook a gourmet dinner for you slaps while you swim ... or whatever it is you're doing," Thor said from behind Aiden.

"Thanks, bro." Aiden was so taken by Melene he couldn't even come up with a proper rebuttal.

Thor laughed heartily at Aiden's expense, but Aiden completely ignored him, his gaze focused where he wanted it to be. On Melene. Here in this beautiful remote spot, with Greer and Thor having set up and now monitoring the security, he could hold and kiss her without the safety concerns.

Only the guilt of knowing someday soon he'd leave her behind should hold him back.

He hid a frown at that nagging thought.

He heard footsteps, Thor's voice prattling on, and finally the back door slid closed behind them. He kicked them toward the shallow end where he could plant his feet and easily hold her close.

Melene blinked prettily up at him. "Thor's hilarious," she said.

"He is."

"Your brothers are both great guys. Well, all of them, really."

"They are." He did not want to talk about his brothers right now.

She tilted her head slightly and her gaze trailed over his face and his shoulders. "But I have to admit that Thor's wrong."

"About what?" He licked his lips, the pressure of her body

against him making him far too warm and a little cloudy in the head. Self-control was essential for him as a Delta and a SEAL. But right now, he was going to let it go and not worry about the fear of the future. He loved the idea.

"You're definitely the most handsome Delta."

He grinned at that. "I'll tell him you said so."

"Don't. He'll spend hours trying to convince me otherwise."

"True." He shrugged. "But I bet we'll have hours waiting here."

"We might." She trailed her fingers through his short hair and made his scalp tingle with a delicious pressure. "But there's something else I'd rather do for hours than listen to Thor claim he's more handsome than you."

His stomach heated up. "Oh? What are you thinking? I'd be happy to accommodate you."

"I hope you will." Her dark eyes were so beautiful he was lost.

"What can I do for you?"

"Kiss me until Thor makes us come eat dinner," she said sweetly.

"Yes, ma'am." He was done fighting his feelings for her.

He let her feet slide to the floor of the pool and wrapped his arms around her lower back, pulling her flush against him. Then he captured her lips with his. Fireworks seemed to explode inside him as she returned the pressure of his kiss and they traded beautiful kisses in the tranquil pool, the birds and a soft wind through the trees their only accompaniment.

When the sliding glass door opened and the delicious smell of savory meat drifted out, he forced himself to release her from the kiss.

"Sheesh," Thor called to them. "Are you two pruned yet? Or maybe your mouths are raw from all that kissing. Get in here and eat. And no, don't you dare ask if you can shower first. It's all hot and ready and no matter how ugly Aiden is, he's my twin and I love him enough to feed him delicious food fresh, not stale and reheated."

Melene laughed and Aiden joined her.

"We're coming," Aiden said. It was torture to release his tight grip on Melene and wade out of the pool.

They wrapped up in towels and endured lots of teasing from Thor. Greer was his normal, non-judgmental self and didn't so much as smirk, wink, or blush as they all consumed the delicious pulled pork and jalapeno jelly on hot rolls with potato, pasta, and green salads. Thor had even made a beautiful chocolate cake with the words 'Happy birthday Thor and Aiden' written on the top.

"What's this?" Aiden asked. "Our birthday was back in June."

Thor gave him the most serious look Aiden had seen in a while. "Do you know how many birthdays I've celebrated without you?"

Aiden was taken aback and had to admit, "I ... haven't kept track."

"I have. Ten. Ten years since we had a birthday in the same location."

Guilt punched Aiden in the gut. He knew his family, particularly his mom and Thor, would love nothing better than for him to settle down in Summit Valley. And Papa would love having a highly-trained special ops soldier to help with the Delta Protection Detail.

He hated to disappoint them, but his path was set. He risked a glance at Melene. She looked sad for both of them, but she also had a lot of understanding in her gaze. She knew how hard it was to be away from family, but feel certain your path was the one you'd been called to. He didn't even want to think about how that equated to him needing to stop kissing Melene nonstop.

"Sorry, bro," Aiden said to Thor, facing his brother again.

"It's okay. I love you and I'm proud of you. Let's eat some cake, then you're going to shower. And please don't waste any time trying to improve your looks. It's hopeless. And then we're watching Sahara."

Aiden laughed. He loved that his brother could get back to teasing in a blink. They used to love watching Sahara as teenagers and both had claimed they were the main character, Dirk Pitt played by Matthew McConaughey. Though they honestly both loved his sidekick, the hilarious Al Giordino, played by Steve Zahn.

They ate cake, showered, and he and Melene snuggled through the movie. All the brothers were stunned she'd never seen it and she laughed in all the right places and admitted it was the "best movie ever" as they all insisted it was.

After the movie, his brothers said their goodnights and headed up to bed. Aiden would've loved to kiss Melene for a few more hours, but he felt an impending doom. He'd experienced it a couple of times before—right before Mike had been killed in Afghanistan and when Esther had been targeted by a psychotic serial killer and Aiden had been too far away to help. He pulled into himself, trying to target what was causing the uneasiness and if he could do anything to prevent what was coming.

"You'd better get some sleep," she said, standing and offering a hand. She'd misread his worries for exhaustion. He was tired, but he'd survived without sleep plenty of times before.

Aiden let her tug him up. He clung to her hand, not ready to lose this sense of home and the thrill and joy of Melene in his life. They walked slowly up the flights of stairs. Neither of them said anything. Aiden wondered where her thoughts were. Was she dreading that they would have to go opposite directions sometime soon? Was she worried about General Phillip finding them again? Was she simply enjoying the fun afternoon and evening they'd had after such a horrific night last night? Was she feeling uncertain like he was and only wanting to kiss some more?

They made it to her bedroom door. She turned and pressed back into the wall, smiling beautifully up at him. "Thank you, Aquaman," she said.

"For?" He leaned in, pressing closer to her and inhaling a light, sweet perfume.

"Protecting me, being there for me." Her voice lowered. "Kissing me."

"I'm thrilled to do all three," he told her. The impending doom would have to wait for now. Thor and Greer would monitor the cameras and sensors, and there had been no alert. He had no doubt his brothers had set everything up correctly and they were safe. The unease he felt wasn't due to someone coming. It was something bigger-picture, more emotional.

She reached up and grabbed his shirt, tugging him against her. "Let's work on number three."

Aiden willingly complied. He took her lips in a long, drugging kiss and was able to forget any unease of fear of the future. When they came up for air, she smoothed his shirt and murmured, "Sorry. I got a little intense there."

"I loved it."

"Aiden?"

"Yes?" Was she going to tell him to kiss her again? Anytime would be his answer.

"Is there any hope of a future ... for us?"

Aiden's gut clenched. He remembered—had it only been yesterday morning?—telling her that there wasn't any hope. He felt like so much had changed since then. Yet had it? Long distance and a relationship with a SEAL would be tough enough, but add in her intense and demanding career and who knew when they'd ever see each other? He'd happily take any FaceTime calls, but never being physically in the same place would probably kill the relationship pretty quickly. He didn't want to let fear and uncertainty rule, but unless one of them got a change in calling from heaven above, he didn't know how to proceed.

He opened his mouth, not even sure what to say. Should he claim they'd make it work? Should he admit he was falling in love with her? Should he tell her she was incredible but they had no future?

A door slammed downstairs and a whoop, then a yell, "Ding dong, the witch is dead!"

Aiden exchanged a look with Melene, but the churning in his gut told him he'd soon get the answer to his apprehension.

Footsteps pounded up the steps and Thor yelled, "Greer! Get your butt out here. You'll want to hear this."

Greer's door opened below as Thor ran up to Aiden and Melene. He grinned at them. "Sorry to interrupt, but I think you'd all like to know ..." He paused dramatically and waited until Greer reached the top steps and raised his eyebrows expectantly. "Just got a call from Papa. General Carl Phillip has been confirmed killed in a training exercise. Ha! Friendly fire got the son of a gun."

Aiden eased back from Melene, stunned, relieved, and oddly sad. This was it. He'd known something was coming. It was a mixed bag of blessing and curse. Phillip was dead. He and Melene's time together was done. He'd known it would come eventually, but ... so soon? She blinked up at him and he could see she was feeling the same.

"Truly? He's gone?" Aiden asked.

"Yep. Poor, poor King Frederick, losing his best support financially and otherwise." Thor seemed unable to wipe the smile off his face. "You know what this means, right, bro?"

"Melene is safe."

"Well yeah, for sure. The bounty has been retracted by Phillip's brother, a Duke of some sort in England. He claims he'd never want to hurt an innocent American, but he obviously doesn't want a bad rap with his own government or the media, or to lose any of his inheritance money. What the Brits don't confiscate or Frederick hasn't already stolen." He winked. "But the best part ... you two can come to my wedding! Mostly importantly, I can get there."

Aiden smiled. "That is awesome news." He was thrilled he could be there for Thor when there were many times he hadn't been. He was happy Melene could go see her family. But he hated the thought of parting ways. No, hate wasn't strong enough. He abhorred the very thought of it.

Please help us through this, please give me the faith that's gotten me through so many hard spots, he begged heaven above. Then he had to quickly add, *And thank you so much for keeping us safe and setting Melene free and freeing the world of evil like General Phillip.*

He stared into her gorgeous dark eyes. She was as conflicted as he was. Neither of them had expected to fall this hard and fast. Could the way they both felt about each other change their future? He didn't know, but he honestly didn't see a different path for either of them than what they'd been walking before he rescued her.

Saying goodbye to her was going to shred him from the inside out. He should start distancing himself now. What a kick in the pants.

Fear not, I am with thee, played through his mind. But what could his faith do in this situation? Faith couldn't get Melene to stop doing charitable missions or him to quit the SEALs. Not when they'd both felt called to their life's paths by heaven above. Faith couldn't magically marry them and give them time to build the deep trust and love they'd need to sustain a challenging marriage with all-encompassing careers in this cynical and physically and spiritually dangerous world.

Fear not? Usually he could find a way to trust, even in the darkest of circumstances. But tonight, he had to admit ... he was terrified of losing Melene.

Chapter Fifteen

Melene had a hard time settling down, but she finally crashed in the early hours of the morning and was able to get a few hours' sleep before they drove to the airport at seven a.m. and took a chartered jet back to Colorado. Thor complained that Aiden had been pacing the room above him all night. Aiden didn't even fire back. She wondered why he hadn't slept, and then he either dozed throughout the flight or pretended to sleep.

She couldn't blame him for being tired after two nights of no sleep and rescuing and protecting her, but oh, how she wanted to have him answer her question. Did they have hope of a future? She couldn't come up with an easy or foolproof scenario for being together, but she didn't want to let him go. She was willing to let go of the fear of what the future might hold and try to carve a relationship with Aiden into her story. She was ready to make him the foundational block of her story, right next to her faith in the

Savior. If only he'd be willing to answer her question and figure out where they could go from here.

They landed at a private airport near Denver and their families surrounded them. Melene was thrilled to hug her parents, her sisters, and her grandmother, but Aiden was far too somber, and he only had time to give her a quick hug and tell her goodbye before they were whisked into separate vehicles with their own families for the drive to Summit Valley. When her parents turned into their home on the east side of the valley and his family's vehicles kept going, she had to stop herself from crying. There had been something in his blue eyes she hadn't liked when he'd said goodbye. She didn't even like the word goodbye. Why not "see you later"?

The next couple of days passed slowly, with no sign of Aiden. It was wonderful to spend a couple days with her family, but she had to neatly sidestep questions about Aiden from her boy-crazy youngest sister Abigail. Worse, she ached for Aiden and couldn't understand why he hadn't come for her. It hurt.

Could their relationship have just been a fling for him? True, the fire had been a quick flame and sometimes those burned out fast, but her feelings for him were stronger than ever.

As she evaluated and reevaluated each moment, especially their kisses, she realized she didn't understand the meaning of "hard to get." She'd been far too willing and probably pushy. She had initiated, or asked for, every kiss they'd shared. He'd told her originally they couldn't have a future and he'd never amended that, despite how wonderful, sweet, and perfect he'd been to her and for her. It all boiled down to him not falling for her like she'd imagined. She knew hurt and pain would be in her future loving a

Navy SEAL. It had been a risk she thought she'd been willing to take. She just hadn't foreseen it would happen this quickly and while they were still in the same zip code.

The evening of Thor and Shelly's wedding finally came. She'd been away from Aiden for close to forty-eight hours. She wasn't trying to whine and complain, but inside she was. Had he been too busy with his family and wedding preparations, or had he not wanted to come for her? Maybe his mom wouldn't let him out of her sight. Who knew? The excuses she conjured up for him seemed thin.

She should praise heaven above that General Phillip was gone and that she was safe. She'd contacted her boss, Avalyn Shaman-Hawk, and they'd chatted for an hour. She loved Avalyn and really appreciated the strings her boss had pulled when she learned a few hours later they'd created an opening in Costa Rica for her.

How interesting that she was going back to Costa Rica. She had a flight scheduled for tomorrow later in the morning.

Unless Aiden convinced her otherwise.

Her shoulders slumped. That didn't seem like it was going to happen. It didn't seem like he'd even try.

She and her family walked onto the gorgeous slope of lawn above the Deltas' glistening mountain lake. The lake was so blue. It reminded her of Aiden's eyes.

She looked around at the towering mountains decorated with pine and aspen trees and breathed in the clean mountain air. It was so beautiful here, but she'd seen many gorgeous settings throughout the world. Costa Rica and Jamaica had been the most beautiful of all, because she'd been with Aiden and the scenery had been only a backdrop. No scenery could beat his handsome face, blue eyes, and perfect body.

There were Deltas rushing around and some chatting or greeting guests, but she didn't see Aiden. All the Deltas were incredibly good-looking with those bright blue eyes. She supposed that was why Thor and Aiden could tease each other mercilessly about being ugly, because they both knew how handsome they were. Had Aiden only been toying with her? Was he like the sailor who had a girl in every port? He romanced women wherever he was stationed and then easily moved on? It didn't feel right, and she'd instinctively trusted Aiden, but maybe she had been bewitched by his protection, his ability to tease and make her feel incredible, and his handsome face and body.

She and her family walked to the rows of white chairs, each tied with a pale blue ribbon. They found seats in the back and Melene was between Gramma Larue and Abigail. The groomsmen started forming a line to the right of the preacher in front of the arched lattice work draping with pale blue ribbon and white roses, lilies, and daisies. Shelly had a simple classic style and Melene liked it. The setting was so gorgeous it needed little decoration.

No Aiden yet. Melene clutched her hands together and cast glances around.

Two men strode from Papa's house and across the grass. Thor and Aiden. Two incredibly handsome men, but one who made her heart stop. Melene gripped the chair underneath her so she wouldn't run at him and fling herself into his arms. He hadn't called. It was definitely a kiss off and she needed to not desperately run to him.

"Ooh, those Delta men are so hot," Abigail whispered, staring at the lineup of well-built men in tailored, dark-gray suits, white shirts, and pale blue ties. "I have to know if you got any alone time with Aiden while he was protecting you. Please, please tell me the truth."

Abigail had begged and begged for details about Aiden and whether Melene had kissed him. Melene had given her nothing, schooling her face and praying she'd stop asking. She had admitted to Jessica privately that she'd kissed him and fallen in love with him. Thankfully, Jessica could keep a secret from the boy-crazy Abigail. Her youngest sister needed to stop drooling over the Deltas, most of all Aiden.

Thor's face was split in a grin. Aiden was smiling happily too, but his gaze was darting around as they approached the wedding party. Unfortunately, the crowd was huge. The entire Summit Valley was probably here, and then there were Thor and Shelly's rodeo friends and some military higher ups if the stars on their uniforms meant something.

Aiden moved into his place right next to Thor, but his gaze kept searching. She wanted to stand up and scream, "I'm here, I'm here." But what if he wasn't even looking for her?

It was an impressive lineup of handsome Delta men. As far as she knew, Colton, Thor, and Greer and were all attached now. Aiden, Chandler, and Hudson were the only Delta men without a match. Could she be Aiden's match, or did he even want one?

He kept searching faces until his blue eyes settled on ... her. Melene couldn't hide the smile that spread across her face. Their gazes got entangled and held, and she was lost in the man she loved. Loved. Really?

Was she that far gone?

Yes, she was.

She had no idea why he hadn't come for her, but somehow he could explain that away. After the ceremony and dinner, they could dance and talk and then sneak away and hug and kiss and plan ... a future? Could they really have a future? Maybe but it would be tough and take a lot of faith, work, and commitment on both of their parts, but she would give it her best effort. Was Aiden interested in that? In her?

"What's up with Aiden?" Gramma Larue said too loudly as the crowd settled into their seats to await the bridesmaids and the bride. "I think you left a few details out of your time together."

Melene's face and neck burned. She said nothing, managing a weak smile when far too many people turned around and stared at them. Sadly, that also broke her concentration on Aiden. Music started and the gorgeous bridesmaids sauntered down the aisle. They were all wearing fitted pale blue satin dresses. Melene's dress was the exact same color, but luckily a different fabric and cut. She hoped nobody thought she was trying to worm her way into the Delta family by dressing in the wedding colors.

A beautiful brunette Melene didn't know walked down the aisle first. Abigail informed her it was Colton Delta's fiancée Bailey. Another gorgeous brunette seemed to bounce happily down the aisle. Melene recognized her from Greer's picture—Emery Reeder, the woman who'd come to avenge her brother's death and fallen in love with his killer. Crazy story, but what an incredible ending. If Emery and Greer could find happily ever after with obstacles like that, couldn't Aiden and Melene? She snuck a look at him. He caught her eye but quickly looked away.

She sighed. Maddie, Jessie, and Alivia Delta came next, and finally Esther, Aiden's sister. They were all so beautiful and the wedding was picture perfect.

The music changed, and they all stood up for the bride. Shelly Vance seemed to glide up the aisle on the arm of her tall, dark-haired brother Klein. She was exquisitely gorgeous in a very simple white satin dress with capped sleeves, a scooped neck, and a long train. The white satin contrasted with her tanned skin and dark curls. She was a radiant bride. The hemline of the dress scooped up to the knees in the front to show off some teal-colored cowboy boots. It was a fabulous personality touch.

Shelly and Thor could obviously only see each other. It was so sweet and made Melene long even more for what she couldn't have.

Aiden seemed to be focused on Shelly, too. That was the way it should be, but how Melene wished he couldn't tear his gaze from her.

The ceremony and dinner went by quickly and everything was beautiful and perfect, and Melene wished Aiden would look at her. She wished even more he'd leave the wedding party and run to her, tell her he couldn't be without her.

The dancing started as the sun set over the mountains. Melene was accosted on all sides by friends of all ages. People she'd known and loved her entire life. It was wonderful to catch up and hug so many people and get so many compliments and blessings and love bestowed on her. But where on earth was Aiden?

She spotted him across the floor, dancing with his cousin Maddie to a fast country song. They were laughing, and he was a pretty great dancer. He had moves that made her mouth go dry.

Him dancing reminded her of doing water aerobics in the pool in Jamaica. She wished she could rewind to that time, even with the million-dollar bounty on her head.

"Clamp your jaw. You're droolin'," Gramma Larue said at her elbow.

Melene closed her eyes and her mouth, clutching a drink of juice in her hand. "Was it that obvious?"

"Sadly, yes." Gramma Larue said hi to someone, then directed Melene away from the crowd. It was growing dark, and they got out of the circle of light as they walked closer to the lake. It was still light enough to see her grandmother's concerned face. "What's going on, love? Did you fall for that handsome military man?"

Melene nodded. There was no use denying it.

"Well, what woman wouldn't? He's an irresistible one, that's for sure. And now he's trying to ditch you?"

Melene tried to smile. She failed. "It's fine, Gramma. We both have all-encompassing careers we feel are our calling, and they take precedence over a normal, settled life. He tried to tell me not to get invested, but you're right, he was too irresistible for me to keep my distance."

"Ah, love." Gramma patted her cheek. "Such an exotic beauty, and a sweetheart clear through. You wouldn't say crap if your mouth was full of it. Learn to complain and roast some-body for me, would you? The hot jerk is breaking your heart in two."

Thankfully, Melene could laugh at that. "I will not roast Aiden, and he's the farthest thing from a jerk. He is hot and incredible, and I owe him my life." At least she had the wonderful memories of his thoughtfulness, all their kisses, and the rest of their time together.

Shelly and Thor caught her eye on the dance floor. Thor made his bride laugh, but then he tugged her close and kissed her thoroughly. Melene was so happy for them, and so miserable for herself. Even Greer was dancing with the beaming Emery. He looked uncomfortable with the dance steps, but his eyes were shining at his girlfriend. It looked like Greer would do anything for her.

Gramma Larue drew in a steadying breath. "Well, you sit here and mope and lie to yourself about why he's not at your side. I'm going to do something about it."

Melene's eyes widened. "Gramma, no. Please. He protected me and was so caring and good to me. He does not deserve to be called out." Even if he was breaking her heart, she'd be forever grateful for all he'd done for her.

Gramma gave her a challenging look, then she darted away faster than Melene had seen her move in years and strode determinedly to the dance floor.

Melene didn't know if she should follow her and try to stop her, probably causing a scene, or if she should go hide somewhere or beg someone to take her home. This would not end well.

She skirted the floor to where Aiden and Maddie were still dancing. She tried to stay in the shadows so he couldn't see she was moving in. Somehow, he sensed her. His gaze darted right to her and it held.

He stopped dancing and Maddie grabbed his arm. "What's wrong ..." She followed his gaze. "Oh." Her own blue eyes became scheming. "Ohhhh," she drawled out.

Gramma Larue reached Maddie and Aiden before Melene could do anything but stare at him.

"Listen up, sailor," Gramma said much too loudly, poking a finger in Aiden's face. It would've been adorable to see her stooped with age, tiny grandmother trying to tell the tough, tall SEAL what was up, if it wasn't Melene who was going to be humiliated when he kindly explained he wasn't interested and never would be. He'd simply been doing his assignment protecting her. What did a few delicious kisses, banter, thoughtful gestures, and fun times in the water mean to a man like Aiden who'd been pursued by women the world over? Tears pricked at her eyes as so many of their interactions flashed before her mind, particularly him taking such tender care of her when she'd been sick and making sure she had toiletries and clothes. What kind of tough guy did that for a woman? How could she mean nothing to him?

"Yes, Mama Larue?" Aiden sweetly bent down and took Gramma's hand.

"Oh, don't you try to be cute with me," Gramma hurled at him.

Other people were stopping dancing and watching the interaction. Ah, shoot. At least the music hadn't screeched to a stop ... yet.

Aiden smiled. His gaze darted to Melene and her heart sped up. "I don't know how else to treat you, Mama Larue," he said kindly. "The entire valley loves you."

"Well." She pushed out her chest and pinned him with a look that Melene hadn't seen since she'd stolen Gramma's stash of Ghirardelli's king-sized chocolate caramel bars and eaten three of them, making herself sick for a day and a half.

"I don't really care if you love me," Gramma said feistily. "I want you to love my girl."

Aiden's blue eyes focused in on her. His mouth opened, but nothing came out. Melene thought the entire wedding party was staring now, but she wasn't about to break from staring at him. All she could see was Aiden.

She clutched her hands together and prayed for ... she didn't know what to pray for. She loved him, but she'd never ask him to leave his career and calling in life, and she couldn't imagine leaving hers. If only they could be like Shelly and Thor and settle down in this gorgeous valley with all these wonderful people. Safe, happy, loved, and creating children and memories together.

Aiden patted Gramma's hand and said without breaking concentration on Melene, "Excuse me, Mama Larue. It was great to see you."

"Great to see you, handsome. Don't mess this up, you hear?"

Aiden nodded, but said nothing.

He released Gramma and strode off the dance floor, across the grass, and to where Melene anxiously waited. Melene's heart was in her throat, and she had no clue if Gramma had just saved her life or doomed her to a future without Aiden.

Chapter Sixteen

Melene studied Aiden's handsome face as he grew closer, but he felt like a stranger to her. Gone were the teasing, easy smiles and longing looks.

Stopping in front of her, he stared down at her broodily. That look on his face didn't seem like her Aiden. His gaze swept over her, and he said huskily, "You look gorgeous, Melene. I love that dress on you."

His words were a compliment, but they felt too formal.

"Thank you," she managed. "You look very handsome." She laughed nervously. "I'm sure Thor would agree."

He finally smiled. "I'm sure he wouldn't."

She laughed again, but even the air felt thick and strained between them. What had happened to them? A few beats passed and the only sound was the music and laughter and talking from the wedding party. She pressed a hand down the side of her dress and his gaze traveled hungrily over her. It made her stomach flutter, but also made her sad. Was she only someone to be beautiful to him, someone to kiss and then discard? She'd assumed their connection was miles deeper than that.

"You chose the perfect color of dress," he murmured, pointing to his pale blue tie.

"I had no idea. I felt a little awkward, like I was trying to be part of the ... family," she managed.

His eyebrows went up. Again, he simply stared at her.

Melene wanted him to smile, to tease, to pull her close, to love her. When she couldn't take it any longer, and it looked like he might just back away and leave her standing there, she burst out, "What happened to us? I thought you cared."

"Ah, Melene." He pushed a hand at her hair and then he took her elbow and murmured, "Do you mind a short walk?"

"That's fine." She'd walk for miles in these uncomfortable heels if it meant being close to him. It hurt that she was so invested in him and he seemed to have already distanced himself from her. What did she expect? He'd never told her there was anything deep between them. His kisses had conveyed that to her, but apparently had meant little to him.

They walked in silence away from the party, along the calm lake's shore until they reached the nearby forest. It was getting darker by the moment, but she could still see his handsome face clearly, and sadly she could still see the angst in his beguiling blue eyes. Aiden wasn't calloused or trying to hurt her. He was as unsure and conflicted as she was, but he was handling it far differently than she wanted him to. He was shutting himself away from her and creating distance before they even had real physical miles separating them.

He released her elbow and turned to her. "I'm so sorry, Melene. These past two days I've wanted to call you ... no, that's a lie." His jaw worked, and he clenched and unclenched a fist.

He was so handsome. It hurt to look at him and know he'd never be hers. He'd said he wanted to call her, but then said it was a lie. Her stomach ached like he'd punched her. Aiden would never physically hurt her, but he was destroying her emotionally.

"The truth is ..." He took a slow breath and Melene dreaded the truth. She wanted to put a finger to his lips, prevent him from making a sound, just like he'd covered her mouth with his hand in the ocean as they'd fled for their lives. Silence and this ache were better than the blow he was about to deliver.

His blue eyes were intense and laser-focused on her as he said, "The truth is, Melene, I've wanted to sprint to your house, pin you against a wall, kiss you until neither of us could breathe, and then beg you to never leave my side again."

Melene's breath rushed out. His words were unexpected and so beautiful. She wanted to throw herself against his chest and start with the kissing, but she had to ask, "Then why didn't you come?"

His blue gaze was tortured. "What would it accomplish besides making me long even more for something I'll never have?"

Her heart seemed to stop, then thud heavily against her chest. "You'll never commit to me?"

He reached up and cupped her cheek. His touch was tender and made her ache for him. "I'll never commit to anyone. I can't leave my life, my calling." He released her face. "I've seen friends try to make a relationship work, but it always ends in pain for them and their wives. Sometimes it's broken their wives emotionally. I can't do that to you."

She blinked at him. Apparently, his fear of their relationship failing had ended it before they could even put forth the faith to try.

Before she could somehow beg him to trust God and trust her and at least try, he gestured almost angrily back toward the wedding party. "Don't you think I'd grab you and hang on forever if I could? Don't you think I want what Thor and Shelly have?" His shoulders sagged and his hand fell to his side.

She knew they'd never have the white picket fence, decorated front porch, and raising their babies next to grandma like Thor and Shelly, but couldn't they be each other's home? Did that even make sense? The problem was, when would they ever be in the same location? Rarely, and she knew it. She noticed he didn't even bring up a long-distance relationship. It would be misery and might even distract him and put him in danger. She'd try it if he would, but she could imagine it wouldn't be nearly enough for either of them and might hurt worse than a clean break.

"I understand," she said. "I can't walk away from my life's calling and I don't expect you to." She hated how unemotional and uninvested she sounded, but she loved him and if never giving their relationship a chance was what he needed, she would let him go.

He studied her. "Walking away from you will be the hardest thing I ever do."

She smiled sadly, but she couldn't help but say, "But you'll do it."

It wasn't a question, so maybe he didn't feel compelled to

answer. He didn't even try. He simply stared at her, misery written all over his face. Melene loved him. She was afraid she'd tell him the truth and make this even harder than it was.

A sob was working its way up her throat, and she was seconds away from breaking down. She never cried for herself. She cried for children who were injured or killed or taken from their loved ones. She cried for mothers who watched their little ones suffer and were ripped apart by their deaths.

Today she wanted to selfishly hide somewhere and sob for the glimpse of happiness she'd been given of her and Aiden and how badly it hurt to know she'd never have him in her life.

Turning, she strode into the forest, not even sure where she was going or if there was even a trail here.

"Melene," Aiden called after her.

She ignored him and kept plunging on. Her tears were blinding her, and her heels were a walking disaster. Her shin painfully connected with a fallen log and she sprawled forward. She would've hit the ground and been even more bruised, except large hands caught her and yanked her against a tall, lean body.

The man smelled of too strong cologne and she tried to yank away, but he held her fast.

Melene looked up into the sharp-angled face and dark, cold eyes of none other than General Carl Phillip. Horror filled her insides like a million icy pinpricks.

"Finally I get you alone, and I didn't even have to pay a million-dollar bounty."

She should've screamed, but all she could gasp out was, "But ... you're ... dead."

He laughed—a cold, fathomless laugh. "Faking a death gives a brilliant, wealthy man so much leeway to create disaster and mayhem."

Understanding made her stomach turn over and nausea crawl up her throat. "You came for me."

"And for the Delta family secret weapon."

"Weapon?" Melene had no idea what he was talking about.

"Isn't that right, Lieutenant Delta?"

Melene tried to pull away again, but she couldn't. She looked over her shoulder and saw Aiden through the murky darkness. Her heart leaped. He'd come for her. Maybe they couldn't be together, but the fierce determination in the lines of his face and body told her he'd never let harm come to her.

"Release her and I *might* make your death less painful," Aiden growled at the man. "No international incident when I skin you alive on my own property."

Melene's eyes widened. She'd never heard Aiden speak so violently, but it was because he cared so deeply for her. It sent a thrill down her despite the desperate situation she was in.

Phillip laughed. "Don't be cheeky with me, squid. You don't have your mates to back you up today, but I do."

Men emerged from behind the trees closest to her and Phillip. Melene gasped and counted eight men who looked like they ate nails for snacks. Shaved heads, well-built bodies, and weapons strapped all over them.

"The wedding was the perfect distraction for me to get around the Deltas' normally secure fortress. Nobody is as tight about security when hundreds of guests have infiltrated your property. But I hope when I kill you it *will* become an international incident. This is how the end of your miserable life is going to play out," General Phillip snarled at Aiden. "You and this beauty are going to come with us. You're going to take me to the weapon and give it to me. Then if you cooperate fully, I'll try to make *your* death less painful while I enjoy my prize." His grip tightened on her.

Melene could hardly catch a breath. She could handle anything they threw her way, but she couldn't let them kill Aiden. What on earth was this weapon they were after? The entire valley knew the Delta family was impressive and some of the family like Aiden, Esther, and Papa Delta were military, but this seemed a league above that. It explained why Thor and Greer knew security and handled their weapons so comfortably and why Papa Delta had easily pulled so many strings with the military to help her.

Aiden's lips curved into a smile. What on earth was he smiling about? "You are such a typical and lame villain, Phillip," he said. "Blustering and wasting time, and giving me plenty of time ..."

"Time for what?" Phillip demanded.

"I'd explain, but unfortunately you're too stupid to catch up. And regrettably, I *do* have to make your death relatively painless," Aiden said.

He yanked out a pistol from his suit coat so fast Melene barely registered what was happening before he fired. The general flew backward, his grip on her relaxing, but not enough. He pulled her off balance. She fell on top of him, his body cushioning the fall.

He didn't cry out, and he wasn't moving. His eyes were sightless, and blood covered his head.

Melene screamed and tried to scramble away.

"Melene!" Aiden rushed toward her, gun in hand.

Phillip's men all had their guns out and pointed at Aiden.

Melene got off the body but froze on her knees, pine needles and rocks poking through her dress.

"Stop!" one of them commanded. "We still have our orders, straight from King Frederick. We're not supposed to kill you until we have the weapon, but we can maim you and make it a miserable walk to wherever you're hiding it. With or without the general, we'll get that weapon, and the woman appears to be a great motivator for you."

"You're even stupider than your general was." Aiden's smile grew. "Your idiot general gave me plenty of time to get my *mates* here."

The trees behind Aiden came alive and Melene's eyes widened as every Delta family member, even the women in their gorgeous pale blue dresses, along with Klein Vance and Sheriff Reed Peterson, edged in to the sides of and behind Aiden. The only ones Melene didn't see were the bride and Colton's girlfriend Bailey.

They all had guns in their hands—some of them just had pistols while others wielded big, scary-looking guns. Melene was in shock. She'd had a few clues, but this confirmed it. The Deltas were obviously not the benevolent, smart, talented, and beautiful people the valley assumed they were.

Aiden gestured back with his head. "I count seventeen to eight. If you like the odds, by all means, take your shot. If you've got enough brains in those small skulls to realize you're going to be slaughtered, because I promise you every one of my family members has better training than you've ever dreamed of having, lay down your weapons. Maybe you can pray whatever government you claim allegiance to will claim you."

Tense seconds ticked by longer than hours. Would the men

back down or would they start a blood bath, not wanting to be arrested or because of their blind allegiance to the murderous King Frederick? Melene couldn't stand the thought of any of the Deltas being injured or killed while she kneeled here, especially Aiden. Her brain scrambled for something she could bargain with to stop Frederick's men from shooting, but she had nothing. Could she at least be a distraction?

She could feel the tension surrounding her. She shot to her feet and held out her hands. "Take me," she begged Frederick's men.

"Melene, no!" Aiden roared.

The men looked at her as if not sure what she was trying to accomplish. Everyone tightened their grips on their weapons as Aiden crossed the feet separating them and stepped in front of her.

"These men are going to set down their weapons and put their hands on their heads," Aiden said in a calm voice that didn't match the fierce look in his blue eyes. "Because they would rather live and hope to be rescued or released rather than die for a lie." He focused on the men. "There is no Delta weapon. General Phillip brought you here because he wanted the most beautiful woman in the world added to his harem. Don't take the fall for his selfishness and join him in purgatory tonight."

A few more beats passed, and Melene prayed the men would listen.

Finally, one by one, the men each held up their free hands and slowly set their weapons down.

"I thought you'd see it that way," Aiden said.

Sheriff Reed and Papa Delta led the way, charging toward the men and herding them back through the forest.

Aiden turned to her and wrapped her up tight in his arms. "Melene," he chastised her. "That was insanely brave; don't you ever do something like that again."

"Okay," she agreed, shaking now that it was all over and the adrenaline rush was leaving her body.

He kissed her forehead and held her tight. She felt safe and loved and ... home.

She knew this changed nothing about their future, but once again Aiden had been her hero, saved her life, and proven himself incredible.

"You're all right?" he asked.

"Yes, thanks to you," she managed. She cupped his face and said, "I know it's stupid and I know we can't be together, but you are my hero and my Aquaman and I love you, Aiden Delta."

Aiden's eyes widened, but luckily he didn't push her away. So she arched up and kissed him.

He kissed her back. The kiss was desperate and all-consuming and as amazing as every kiss they'd shared. Sadly, as it slowed down, she could feel it was a kiss of farewell.

Someone whistled and there was some laughter around them, but Melene ignored everyone but Aiden.

He rested his forehead against hers, and even in the dark, she could see the intensity of his blue eyes. "I love you too, Melene," he said in a deep, wonderful voice.

She licked her lips, so lost in him, wishing they could kiss again. "But it changes nothing about our future, does it?"

He didn't say anything for a beat, then his voice was gravelly as he managed, "Just makes it more painful."

Melene closed her eyes. She couldn't take it anymore. He was her hero, her perfect fit, the love of her life, her home ... and he could never commit himself to being hers.

She softly kissed him again, but pulled back before he could return it. "Thank you, Aquaman. Thank you for holding my hair and cleaning up my puke, thank you for clothing the naked and providing a toothbrush, thank you for making me laugh and playing in the water like little kids, thank you for rescuing me and protecting me, thank you for kissing me more wonderfully than I have ever been kissed, thank you for giving me the best five days of my life. I will never stop praying for you. I will never stop loving you."

He smiled sadly throughout her speech. "I'll do the same."

Melene pulled from his embrace and stumbled away from him. He reached out as if to steady her, but she couldn't handle him touching her again or she'd fall to her knees and beg him to let her follow him around like a Navy SEAL Aquaman groupie.

She pushed his hand away and made her way through the forest toward the wedding. Luckily, someone had brought a light to illuminate the area, and she'd only made it a few steps before the groom himself was at her side. She'd never seen Thor so serious. He took her arm and helped her around a boulder, then over a log.

He glanced back at his twin and Melene couldn't stop herself from looking as well. Aiden was tall and beautiful and perfect. The light showed his blue eyes, handsome face, and tough figure to their advantage. Sadly, he looked like the tortured hero as he watched her, not her teasing Aquaman at all. She hated it. She hated leaving him. But he'd chosen this.

"Poor simp," Thor murmured. "This is going to break him, you know?"

Melene kept walking and Thor kept up. "He was the one who insisted we could never be."

"I know. Stupid, ugly idiot anyway. If it wasn't my wedding, I'd punch that pathetic look off his face."

Melene wanted to laugh at that. There was nothing stupid, ugly, or idiotic about Aiden Delta. He was a hero and the best man she knew. She risked one more look and was afraid she'd never be able to get the picture of his blue eyes looking tortured out of her head.

How she loved him.

How she hated their tragic love story.

Chapter Seventeen

Aiden was back with his team and doing training exercises at their home base in Virginia two days after Thor's wedding. His friends were thrilled to see him again. And within an hour, they were grumbling about how he wasn't himself and what had happened to him.

An excruciating week went by. No Melene. No sign of Melene.

He would've laughed at himself, but he was too miserable. What did he expect? Did he think she was going to come to him when she'd told him she loved him, thanked him so beautifully, and he hadn't even tried to figure out a future? This was on him, but he had no idea how to change it.

He prayed desperately every night for a solution and he avoided Thor's calls, responding to every text his brother sent with: *Enjoy your honeymoon and stop worrying about me.*

Aiden worried about himself. He worried a lot. Should he

retire from the SEALs? Should he beg her to give up her career? Should he have Papa get him another leave of absence to focus on protecting the Delta secret and fighting King Frederick privately now that everything seemed to be escalating that way?

A few hours after dinner on day twelve without hearing Melene's sweet voice, touching Melene's soft skin, laughing with Melene, or seeing her beautiful face, Jace found him on the shooting range. He waited while Aiden finished his rounds with his Glock and then leaned against the table. The range was quiet and the sky deepening around them.

Aiden had shared far too much of the story with his close friend. Jace hadn't judged him or told him he was wrong. He'd commiserated and his exact words had been, "At least you weren't as deep as I was, and hopefully it won't mess you up for as long."

Now Aiden could feel Jace had something important to tell him. Hopefully they were getting deployed and were going to secretly hunt down Frederick and riddle his pathetic body with bullets.

"Just because I messed up Charisse like I did doesn't mean you'd do the same to Melene," Jace said in the softest voice Aiden had ever heard from his CO.

Aiden drew in a breath. Not an assignment to take out a dictator. Dang.

"I know that," he admitted. "Our story would be different, but ... the odds are more than against us, Jace."

Jace looked at him, and then he laughed. "When has the brave, laugh in the devil's face, so full of faith in God he tattooed scripture on his back, Aiden Delta ever cared if the odds were against him?"

Aiden could only blink at him. Jace was right. Usually, he liked the odds against him so he could push himself harder.

"You're scared. Plain and simple. To borrow an expression from Thor, 'Cowboy up, you ugly loser.'"

"Oh, great. Now you're quoting Thor."

"Yep. And he's on the phone for you." Jace extended his cell. "Said you won't answer his calls and he doesn't think you're even reading his texts."

Aiden rolled his eyes. He wasn't getting away from being called out tonight. He "cowboyed up" and extended his hand. Jace put the phone in it and slapped him on the shoulder. "I'll be there for you, buddy. Whatever you decide."

"Thanks." Aiden appreciated his friend and CO's support. "That means a lot."

Jace nodded and walked away.

Aiden drew in a breath and put the phone to his ear. He didn't even need to say hello.

"You ugly fool," Thor shot at him. "What happened to my twin? The man I respect more than any other? You wussed out and ditched the love of your life?"

"Good to hear from you, too. How was the honeymoon?"

"Brilliant, perfect, amazing. If you want to feel even more miserable, lonely, and dejected than you do right now, I'll give you a play-by-play."

"Please don't." Aiden wandered along the gun range, grateful no one was here. "Spit it out so you can get back to Shelly."

"All right. Listen up, and I mean it. This isn't a 'pay half attention to the preacher's sermon.' This is 'the world's ending and you need every bit of inspiration you can from this speech or you'll end up on the devil's side.' You got me?"

Aiden actually laughed. "I got you."

"Here we go. Jace is right. Lieutenant Aiden Delta, tough Navy SEAL and twin to the most impressive, handsome, and driven cowboy on the planet, doesn't care about the odds. You'd choose the risk in any other situation, and you'd have the faith to go forward no matter what if it helped somebody else."

Aiden knew that was true.

"For the first time in your life, be a selfish bugger," Thor said to him.

"Excuse me?" The Deltas had been raised to be unselfish and to put God, family, country, and the secret first. It was in his DNA.

"This is the time to be selfish. To do what's right for you. What's right for Melene. I want you to prove that you trust in heaven above and I want you to choose the risk of loving and losing. Honestly, bro, what could be scarier than missing out on loving Melene?"

Aiden thought about that. He wasn't scared of any battle or any man, but missing out on Melene? That was terrifying. But hurting her was even more terrifying.

"She'll end up hurt and alone," Aiden fought back. "You can't expect me to be selfish enough to do that to her."

"Holy crap, bro, see this clearly. She's hurting and alone right now. How do you justify that?"

Aiden swallowed. He had no response for that.

"You two have a connection that only comes once in a lifetime. You found someone who makes you feel at home no matter where in the world you are."

Aiden was impressed that his teasing brother had seen and felt all of that from his and Melene's interaction. It was all true.

"Let the fear of the unknown go and realize your calling in life can change and adapt. God will make it work out for you and those you're supposed to help with your specialized skills, talents, bravery, and faith." Thor drew in a breath. "But dang it all to heck, Aiden, don't miss out on Melene. Go to her. Figure it out. You'd fight for the underdog. You'd fight for the underprivileged. You'd fight for me. Go fight for the woman you love."

Aiden clung to the phone. He stopped pacing. Thor was breathing quickly after his speech. Aiden felt it all deeply, but he had no clue how to respond.

"Okay, that's all I've got. If that beautiful speech doesn't get through your thick skull, you're uglier and stupider than I thought. Wait, wait, wait, there's one more thing. Do you believe that scripture you tattooed on your back or not? Fear not. Have faith. I love you, bro."

Thor hung up.

Aiden was thankful his brother hadn't demanded a response. He put the phone in his pocket and kept pacing as the night deepened around him. He had no clue how late it was when he hit his knees. Faith not fear. Only his Father above could give him answers now.

Chapter Eighteen

Melene spent two weeks experiencing a very different side of Costa Rica than the gorgeous house and fun-filled afternoon and evening she'd spent with Aiden here. She was on the coast, which was beautiful, and she loved spending time in the warm ocean waters. It was drier here and not as green as the cloud forest she'd been close to with Aiden. She was helping in a refugee camp that Health for All sponsored. The refugees were mostly from Nicaragua, fleeing political unrest and seeking to make a better life in the more affluent and stable Costa Rica.

She lifted her long ponytail off her neck and fanned her hand at herself to cool the sweat. Looking longingly at the nearby ocean, she let the soothing sound of the waves wash over her. She wished she could jump in and swim. She really wished her Aquaman would rise up out of that ocean. Silly.

She hadn't heard from Aiden. Not that she'd expected to. After everything had calmed down the night of Thor's wedding and General Phillip's attack, she'd tried to get some answers out of Sheriff Reed about the Delta weapon, but he'd given her nothing. He'd told her if she cared for the Delta family, she should stop asking questions and definitely not spread any rumors. She assured him she did care for all of them, one in particular, and she'd cease and desist. She didn't need to know some secret. She needed Aiden.

She'd finally gone home late that night and tossed and turned in her old bedroom. Then her family had driven her to Denver the next day. They had eaten a nice long breakfast together and had seen her off at the airport.

She was glad to be back. She loved her work and she loved the children. She was making a difference and fulfilling her life calling, and that was what mattered.

But she was so miserable without Aiden.

What options did she have? He'd never seemed open to any. If he would've asked her to leave her work and follow him around, would she have done it? Could a spouse even follow a Navy SEAL around? Maybe the spouse could live on a whatever Navy base the SEAL was stationed at and see them as much as possible.

She let out a frustrated growl. Aiden hadn't even asked her to pursue any kind of relationship, and here she was trying to figure out how to be his wife. So dumb.

She looked longingly at the ocean. The calm waves broke on the sand and some children were digging in the sand a hundred yards down the beach. She could also see some snorkels over by the reef, but no Aquaman rising out of the waves. No hero coming to carry her back into the water. She'd worked hard not to be overly emotional and had never thought of herself as a romantic. Her longing for Aiden was turning her into a ... would Thor call it a simp? She wasn't even sure what that meant, but she assumed a hopeless case who would do anything to be with the person they loved.

"Melene?" a young voice asked. A sweet girl with large, dark eyes tugged at her hand. "You okay?"

She smiled brightly. "Of course, sweetheart. Now, is that speedy-fast brother of yours going to race me again?"

Talia's older brother, Tyrell, approached them and rubbed his hands together. "I'm gonna win this time."

The children's English was remarkable and Melene had been working with a group of them for countless hours to improve it. Most of the parents only spoke Spanish, and they were also usually full of encouragement for their children to work with Melene and become fluent in English. It could change the entire family's future for the children to eventually find English-speaking jobs or go on to higher education. When the children were with Melene, they only spoke English. The foot races, and occasionally playing in the ocean, were breaks that helped them physically as well as mentally.

"Wait." Tyrell held up his hand. "What about a new race?"

Melene smiled. "What's a new race?"

"In the water." Tyrell pointed.

"You don't know how to swim." She pointed out the obvious. She'd tried to teach him, but she didn't have the talent for teaching like Aiden did. Ah, Aiden. She could feel his hands on her as he instructed her to improve her swimming strokes, see him grinning at her.

She'd happily go into the ocean today, even if Tyrell's swimming didn't improve. The salty sea could welcome her like Aiden's arms. Sadly, nothing compared to Aiden's arms.

"I can't swim," Tyrell admitted. "But he can." Tyrell pointed again, a huge smile on his cute face.

Melene pivoted and stared. She was shocked to see a man rising up out of the water. The exact man she'd been longing to see for the past two weeks. Chills popped up on her arms and her heart sped up. Was this real or a mirage?

Aiden took out his regulator and pulled his mask off his face. He had an oxygen tank on his back but no shirt on. His beautiful chest, shoulders, arms, abs, and the tattoo on his chest were on perfect display, glistening with drops of water and the sun shining off of him as if he really were Aquaman.

His blue eyes sparkled happily at her, and Melene's stomach flipped over as her pulse took off at a gallop.

"Aiden!" she screamed.

She ran across the beach as he pushed toward her through the water. He slid the oxygen tank to the sand, dropped his other gear, and caught her in his arms.

He swung her around, then bent and kissed her. He tasted of salt and every good dream she'd ever had. He kissed her very, very thoroughly and Melene knew ... she didn't need a home base. She didn't need anything but Aiden. Her Aquaman was her home. They could live in the ocean for all she cared. They'd work things out with their life callings, they'd carve out a future somehow, but most importantly, they'd have faith and savor every moment.

Could she convince him to give them a chance? If not, why was he here?

They pulled back to catch a breath. Melene could hear a lot of chattering and movement behind her at the camp. They were probably drawing a crowd, but she didn't care. Aiden was here, and she wasn't looking away from those blue eyes and that handsome face.

"What are you doing here? Did you set that up with Tyrell?" She had so many questions, and those two didn't seem the most important after she spit them out.

He only grinned and cradled her in close. "I spent twelve long, miserable days aching for you," he said and she trembled, her smile getting a little watery. "Then Jace and Thor both cussed me out and Thor gave me quite the speech." He laughed. "Basically, he said to choose faith, not fear, and that you are my home. The rest will work out if we trust in God."

Melene's heart clutched. That was exactly what she'd been thinking.

"So I had Papa do his 'I'm such an important ex-Admiral thing' and I'm officially on extended leave from the SEALs and planning to follow you around like a puppy dog until there's a mission that Jace can't accomplish without me or the Delta family needs me to help protect the secret. But what matters most is that we're together for as long as we can be and we figure out how to make it all work—"

Her body felt light and happy and she loved everything he said, but she had to stop him. "Now wait a minute. You have no idea how much I want my Aquaman following me around like a puppy dog."

He winked. "It'll be fun times."

She laughed. "But Aiden, you love the SEALs and your team and Jace ..."

"I do. But Melene, you're more important than anyone else on this earth to me. Being close to you is the only home I'll ever need."

"Oh, my." Tears sprang to her eyes, and she had to kiss him again. For a very, very long time.

When they pulled apart, she managed, "Thank you, Aiden. I ..." She was crying, and she didn't want to get caught up in the emotion. She never let herself get emotional, but this was her Aquaman. It touched something deep inside that he was saying the words she'd never dreamed he would say, and he definitely meant them. She loved him so much. "First of all ..."

"You already did a *first of all*," he teased.

"Don't you sass me," she threw back at him.

He laughed and lifted her off the ground, spinning her around. "I love you, Melene Collier," he called out.

The crowd cheered at that declaration.

Melene was so full of happy bubbles she was afraid she'd burst. He set her down and kissed her tenderly. "I love you, Aquaman," she told him.

He grinned and then he asked, "Okay, I'll stop teasing you. Second thing?"

"What on earth is the Delta secret? Some weapon?"

His gaze got serious, and he looked around quickly. Even though her friends were giving them plenty of distance and had only reacted when he yelled he loved her, he lowered his voice and leaned close to her ear. "It's kind of a long story, but the Delta family is sworn to protect a secret hidden in a cave above my family's valley."

Her eyes widened. "Is it a weapon?" she asked quietly, remembering General Phillip's words.

"I honestly don't know. One of my siblings or cousins will be tasked as Secret Keeper whenever Papa decides. Maybe he's already chosen one of them. But only the Secret Keeper knows the secret. Prevents the rest of us giving away information under duress."

Her eyes widened. "Why wouldn't you be Secret Keeper?"

"Papa told Colton and I years ago we wouldn't. Too obvious." His brow furrowed. "And maybe not being Secret Keeper is no insurance. Alivia and Klein have been kidnapped. Thor and Shelly were attacked. Remember how Greer killed Emery's brother?"

She nodded, shocked by all this info, but at least she was in Aiden's arms. She could handle anything if she was in his arms.

"Well, the reason Emery's brother almost killed Alivia was to force her to take him to the secret. Greer also had to protect Emery and kill the man who sent Travis and his guys after the secret."

Her stomach was doing crazy things that had nothing to do with the romance and joy of Aiden being here. "So this secret's a pretty big deal."

"Yes. Like a saving-the-world kind of big deal. My entire family is committed to keeping it safe." He looked her over. "Are you having doubts about marrying me because of it?"

"Aiden Delta!" She could not believe him. "I would marry you if you had warts growing out of your nose and we had to live on the river in Jamaica next to that crocodile."

He smiled.

"But you haven't even asked me properly, and I have no idea what our future holds."

"God will help us work the future out," he reassured her. "All that matters is we're together, and we trust in Him. Fear not."

She felt that deeply. "You're right. I'll trust you and I'll trust God."

They were quiet, and then he gave her a tender kiss.

"And the proposal?" she asked sassily when the kiss ended.

He laughed. "Sadly, I haven't had time to get a ring, but I will remedy that soon." His brow furrowed. "In Jamaica ,when we were waiting for Thor and Greer and the helicopter, did you realize we were on an old sugar plantation?"

"No, but that makes sense."

"I remember looking at the foundation of the home and thinking about how the plantation owners and the slaves who fought for their freedom and all the stories those foundations could tell. Those people are gone, but they probably left a legacy behind of family and traditions and memories and even footings of their home. It made me sad that I have no legacy to leave behind."

"You've done so much good in this world," Melene interrupted. "You can't think that."

"Thank you, and I know people would honor me for a hero's death, and my family would mourn me, but maybe I'm getting old." He smirked. "I want a legacy, a family, children." His voice deepened. "Children with you."

She beamed at the vision of their future family.

"Most of all, I want you by my side for whatever life throws at us and whatever adventures, joys, heartaches, and lessons come our way. We can share adventures, the philanthropist life, the military life, life in Summit Valley. Wherever we go, whatever mission either of us need to do, our legacy will be our love and fighting to be together and having faith that we will be together, in this life or the next."

Melene trembled from his sweet words and blinked, but the tears still spilled over.

Aiden tenderly wiped a tear away with the pad of his thumb and then murmured, "Will you marry me, Melene? Will you choose faith, let me love you and protect you, and build a legacy together?"

"Yes," she managed.

He bent and kissed her. When he pulled back, he lifted her into his arms and she thought he'd carry her up to the camp and meet her friends. Instead, he turned and carried her into the ocean.

Melene laughed and waved at the crowd, then wrapped her arms around his neck. "We'll be back soon," she called. "Aquaman needs a dip in the salt water."

Several of the people laughed, though most just looked confused as they either didn't speak English or had never seen the movie.

Aiden kept pushing until he was waist deep, then he grinned at her. "Do you trust me?"

"With my life," she said solemnly.

"Oh, good."

Then he leaped and submerged them both in the water. Melene came up sputtering and laughing. She trusted him to protect her, love her, tease with her, comfort her, and make her happy.

She was finally in the arms of her Aquaman. Maybe they'd focus on her career for a while, maybe his next. Maybe they'd go home and protect the Delta secret, or maybe they'd never leave the salty waters of the sea. The unknown was exciting and didn't need to be solved.

All that mattered was that they were together now, and they wouldn't waste a moment enjoying that time and building their legacy of love. When they had to be apart, they'd keep choosing faith over fear and they'd never stop loving each other.

Fear not; I am with thee ...

God was with them, and with Him on their side, they could overcome anything.

Endangered - Excerpt

Kylee Seamons scurried through the stadium gates of Veterans Memorial Stadium, checking over her shoulder to see if she'd shaken her tail.

The answer was a horrifying no.

The lean man with a shaved head and eerie pale blue eyes stayed just close enough to keep her in his sights. She thought she'd lost him several times on the drive from Chicago to Boston, but he always turned up.

He caught her staring, and turned away as if he were heading toward the Korean War Memorial.

Her stomach churned, and not because she'd subsisted on jerky, Snickers, and Red Bulls for the past sixteen hours. Had her shadow been sent by her grandmother, or did King Frederick's man know what she'd overheard? They'd been speaking in Polish and probably assumed if someone overheard them, they couldn't understand them.

Mimi, as her grandmother demanded Kylee call her, because she was "far too young and beautiful" to be called Grandmother, hadn't known Kylee was coming by that night. Kylee got cussed regularly for not stopping by. She prayed for strength and felt prompted to go right then, thinking maybe Mimi would be gone or something. It wasn't easy to endure the berating of Mimi and the attempts to counteract the diatribe from her grandfather, but they were her only family.

She hadn't meant to sign her own death warrant by visiting them last night.

With all the plastic surgery she'd endured over the years Mimi certainly didn't look old enough to be the grandmother of a twenty-seven year old linguist and educator. She loathed the fact that Kylee had a figure curvier than Jennifer Lopez's and people often said she looked like a younger version of the famous actress. Mimi found something to fault about Kylee no matter if she downplayed her curves, starved herself, or tried to stay in the shadows.

Kylee understood her frustrations. She exercised every day and tried to eat right, but she couldn't budge the scale or get rid of her generous curves. She'd tried to stop eating ice cream for over a year but that just made her as miserable as visiting Mimi. If she had any extra money maybe she would hire a personal trainer and a dietitian. The inner-city school district in Chicago she worked at couldn't pay her any more, no matter how expensive living in the city was, and Kylee was diligent about saving. She refused to be reliant on anyone, most especially Mimi, and was prepared for every rainy day.

There was no one taking money at the gate of the classic

stadium in Quincy, Massachusetts just south of Boston. The lacrosse game had started an hour a half ago and it had to be in the fourth quarter. Kylee was only grateful she'd made it, and said a quick prayer in her head to thank the good Lord. When she'd thought of this plan as she escaped Chicago late last night she hadn't known how it would work out, but Chandler Delta was the name that kept coming to her head as she prayed. She hoped it wasn't just her ten-year obsession with the incredible athlete that women the nation over would give up chocolate, or possibly even ice cream, for one date with.

Kylee had actually kissed the superstar, multiple times, back when they were sixteen. She wasn't sure that it counted as a relationship to him but she'd spent the week in Colorado falling in love with Chandler. She'd never forgotten the kisses and connection. Though Chandler had easily written her off and forgotten her.

Chandler had developed into an irresistible man, just ask all his dates, and a lacrosse superstar. Though Kylee was admittedly fascinated with him, she couldn't believe she was dropping her pride from being ghosted by him all those years ago, and coming to him for protection for not just her but the entire country. Apparently she had no pride, but Mimi could've told her that.

She heard a roar go up in the bleachers. At least the lacrosse game wasn't over yet. She didn't know what she would've done if she'd missed him. She had to find Chandler, pretend she was a rabid female fan, well that wasn't much of a stretch. She prayed he recognized her and wouldn't sic security on her before she had a chance to whisper her secrets. Then she could disappear with a clean conscience.

It had been too late to withdraw her savings before she fled Chicago. She should probably hit an ATM since Creepy Eyes seemed to know where she was regardless. Luckily she had over five grand in cash she'd hidden in apartment drawers. She'd used cash instead of credit cards for gas and food driving here to not give Mimi a trail to follow. Turned out that had been a waste as Mimi's man, or whoever Creepy Eyes was, had stuck to her like glue.

Admiral Davidson "Papa" Delta, Chandler's grandfather, would've told her he and his family would protect her and sent someone for her, she knew he would. After the last time she'd contacted Papa Delta, she'd suspected someone was watching her. So either they were tapping her phone or Papa's. This secret had to be shared in person.

She instinctively knew she could trust the Deltas, but she couldn't wait for Papa to extract her. Grandpa Seamons had shown up at her apartment late last night, two hours after she overheard the fateful conversation. He confided that someone was being assigned to eliminate her and she needed to disappear. He wouldn't tell her who had assigned the hit. He'd offered protection, but she didn't know if she could trust even her own grandfather.

When she'd contacted Papa Delta, her grandfather's lifelong friend, the ex-Admiral already had suspicions about her admiral grandfather. But neither of them had known at that point it was her grandmother who was the evil linchpin. Kylee should've guessed, having known for years her snarky grandmother was capable of dark deeds. Though Grandpa was a decisive and accomplished military leader, he was a controlled wimp in his own home.

The question was: Was Grandpa in league with Mimi or not? She loved her grandfather and prayed he was innocent.

She shuddered at the fear and all the unanswered questions. Sick that she hadn't been able to shake Creepy Eyes and wondering when he'd try to "eliminate" her or if he was waiting to see what she did, and who she contacted, first. She'd driven the fourteen hours from Chicago to Boston only stopping for food, drinks, gas, the bathroom, and a two-hour nap. She was exhausted and terrified.

Please help me get the info to Chandler then if it be thy will let me escape, she prayed. She'd been so confused that she'd prayed last night and received the prompting to go to Mimi and Grandpa's at that moment, but now she believed it was for a higher purpose. She could prevent so many deaths by getting the information into the right hands. Her own life was inconsequential at this point. That thought made her gut wrench and cold fear prick on her skin but she had to be brave and not think about being shot in the back at any moment.

Walking through a portal and into a lower section of bleachers, she took in the beautiful scene of a green turf field with thick trees surrounding the bleachers. It was only September eighteenth but some of the trees were changing to red, gold, and burnt orange.

The fast-paced game of lacrosse captured her attention and for a brief moment she watched the action as the Boston Cannons in their navy blue uniforms with red accents controlled the ball with quick passes, progressing closer and closer to the goal against some team that had white and green uniforms.

Three passes were drilled so fast from one player to the next her eyes were still catching up as number eighty-three, the talented Chandler Delta, fired at the goal. The white ball stung the back of the net, passing over the goalie's right shoulder so fast he reacted a fraction of a second too late.

The crowd went insane and Kylee found herself screaming along with them. She loved this game. She'd never been much into sports growing up, but on her one trip to Summit Valley Colorado as a teenager, the irresistibly handsome and charming Chandler Delta had converted her into a lacrosse junkie. He'd taught her how to pass and catch with a lacrosse stick, and he'd taken her on "walks" into the forest where they'd shared some incredible kisses. She knew it had only been a fun fling for him as he'd promised to call and text then never once tried to contact her after she went home with her parents and grandparents to Chicago. Her parents had been killed shortly after and that summer trip and the carefree, romantic, and tantalizing time with him Chandler seemed to live in her mind as the best moments of her life.

She'd watched almost every college game he played at Syracuse and professional games with the Boston Cannons. He was amazing.

"And Chandler Delta stings top shelf to make the score twelve to seven with only two minutes left in the fourth."

As the crowd continued to scream, Kylee looked over her shoulder but didn't see Creepy Eyes. She eased along the bleachers and annoyed quite a few fans as she excused herself past clapping hands as they cheered and then past knees and feet as they settled back down to watch the next face-off. She pushed as far as she dared and finally created a spot for herself in the fourth row. She fastened her gaze on Chandler and found watching him play in real life was even more amazing than watching it on her computer.

The last two minutes of the game wound down far too quickly and as the crowd counted down from ten reality slammed back into her. She wasn't here to ogle the gorgeous superstar, she had to get him a very important message. Fingering the expensive jade and diamond necklace hidden under her blouse that her grandfather had given her, she worried that Grandpa was as rotten as Mimi.

You're the rotten traitor, Mimi's voice said in her head.

Kylee pushed that away and focused on Chandler. She had no clue how she was going to get to him and how she was going to whisper secrets in his ear. She couldn't have Creepy Eyes turn his sights on Chandler.

The buzzer sounded and the crowd exploded with cheers. Some people immediately were heading for the exits. Quite a few others lingered, like Kylee. The rest of the fans were probably reluctant to relinquish the great feeling of a victory with their team, or maybe hoping the players would come talk to them.

Kylee prayed for some way to get Chandler's attention. Would he even remember her? She was an obsessed fan girl of his, but it had been years since they'd seen each other and she'd put on twenty pounds. *Thirty,* Mimi's snarky voice said in her head. *Quiet,* she begged. Keeping a positive attitude as a shapely girl in a thin-obsessed world was next to impossible, but she kept on trying. Her mom and dad had believed she was the most beautiful, smart, hardworking, and charming person on the planet. When they were killed in an airplane accident, she'd had to endure the last two years of high school living with Mimi. Grandpa Seamons had tried but nobody could overcome the snark and digs Mimi was capable of. How she missed her parents.

The Boston players started jogging around the stadium, slapping hands with the fans who surged down to the edge of the bleachers, hanging over the side for a chance to interact with their superstars.

Kylee's stomach hopped. This was exactly the opportunity she needed and had been praying for during the long hours of driving, and hoping she was making the right move.

Looking around for Creepy Eyes, she still didn't see him. She climbed over the three rows in front of her, and pushed her way between two teenage boys to somehow get Chandler's attention.

"Hey," one of the boys protested.

"Sorry," she said, giving him a desperate smile. "I have a huge crush on Chandler Delta."

He grinned back at her. He had her by half a foot but that didn't mean much as she was only five-four because of her four-inch heels. As her grandmother would be happy to remind her, she was probably exaggerating her height just like she downplayed her weight.

"Lucky dude," the kid said. "You could have a huge crush on me."

She couldn't help but laugh. She was disheveled, her hair in a sloppy bun and her blouse and skirt wrinkled. She couldn't imagine she looked attractive right now. It was embarrassing as she wished she could look her best for Chandler, but that wasn't the mission right now.

"Well thank you, sweet boy but I think I'm about ten years older than you."

"You're so beautiful I'm sure age wouldn't come between us." He winked and she thought he was adorable. "Has anybody ever told you, you look like J. Lo?"

"I've heard that before." She was impressed he knew who J. Lo was. Wasn't Jennifer Lopez in her fifties? "I've always wanted a younger brother," she told him,

His nose wrinkled. "Gross. I don't want to be your brother. I want to take you out."

Players started surging past and she had to ignore her crazy but complimentary teenage friend to make sure she didn't miss Chandler. Sometimes her high-school age students hit on her and it always made her laugh. Silly kids were just trying to get extra help or a better grade. She wasn't sure what this kid's excuse was, but she appreciated the bolster to her confidence as Chandler was approaching.

Her heart seemed to stop then take off at a gallop and her palms got sweaty. She completely missed the hands of the two players before him, so focused on those incredible blue eyes, that irresistible grin, and his handsome face. His dark hair was mussed from his helmet and his jersey was drenched in sweat. She didn't mind. Maybe the fact that he wasn't clean and perfect would help him forgive that she wasn't.

She shook her head. It didn't matter. She had to discreetly get him alone, share the conversation she'd overheard, and then find a way to St. Lucia, the Caribbean island of her dreams, where Mimi and her hitman would hopefully never find her.

Kylee could hardly catch a full breath as Chandler got closer to her. He was right there. It was all she could do to not scream his name and beg him to help.

Chandler stopped a couple people away from her and cocked his head at a gorgeous, tall blonde. "Excuse me?" he said kindly, seeming like he sincerely wanted to hear what his fans were saying.

She leaned over the railing and begged him, "Can I have your jersey ... please?"

A couple other players streamed around him, laughing and obviously not wanting to wait. "Chandler, always the ladies' man," a huge redhead said to the shorter dark-haired guy.

"I'll give you my jersey," the dark-haired guy called to the blonde.

She ignored him, drooling over Chandler like every other woman in the stadium.

Kylee's stomach took a nosedive, along with all of her romantic and never to be fulfilled dreams of Chandler being her someone special.

"Sure," he said, gifting the blonde with his charming grin.

He whipped off his jersey and handed it over. The blonde clutched the sweaty thing to her chest. Gross.

Kylee's gaze was drawn to Chandler's chest, partially visible under the small chest pad, and his shoulders and abs that were clearly visible. Oh, my, goodness! She, along with probably ever other female in the stadium, let out a gasp at the sight of all that muscular gorgeousness. It wasn't fair for one man to be that appealing. Kylee had to remember she'd never be the type to date a perfect model athlete. From her social media stalking of his name she'd seen Chandler on dates with so many beautiful women it could make her sick enough to not want to eat ice cream that night. Luckily she overcame that awful impulse. She could use a generous serving of Rocky Road right about now.

"Do you want my shirt?" the blonde asked Chandler coyly.

Kylee's stomach turned over. Nope. She was too sick for even ice cream.

Chandler held up his hands and stepped back. "No thanks."

He moved on to the teenager right in front of her, slapping the kid's hand. His teammate flirted with the blonde about taking his jersey.

"Hey man," Chandler said. "Thanks for coming."

"You're the best!" the kid called out.

"Do you play?" Chandler asked and Kylee's heart softened to him again. How cute was he to give this kid some attention.

"Yeah man, I'm a d-pole for Quincy High."

"Awesome. I'm going to make one of your games this spring. I love watching Quincy play."

"Do you mean it?"

"For sure, man." Chandler was so confident and kind. Kylee had been half in love with him for years. If he kept this up she'd fall the rest of the way and earn a "Stalker Chick" badge for her obsession. It was idiotic to love a confirmed ladies' man, but rational thought went out the window with him this close.

"Keep working hard," Chandler said.

"I will!"

Chandler moved to slap the next person's hand. Hers. It was surreal to have those blue eyes focus in on her. The world started spinning. She reached out her hand, needing to speak and quietly beg him to remember her and to meet her somewhere. She couldn't make her mouth form words and feared he'd slap her hand and keep on moving.

He didn't slap her hand. He wrapped his hand around hers.

His eyes lit up and his generous mouth curved in a happy smile. "Kylee!"

Kylee blinked at him. "You remember me?" she managed to get out in a squeaky voice.

"Of course I remember you. What are you doing here? Don't you live in Chicago?"

She nodded dumbly, cleared her throat, and said, "I need you."

His eyes seemed to grow warmer and his hand clasped hers tighter. "Oh, yeah?" he asked in a husky voice that made her hot from head to toe.

"Get in line, girlie," the blonde yelled at her from a few seats over.

Kylee's eyes widened in horror. It was one thing to be an obsessive fan girl but quite another to let Chandler see that. "Not like that," she tried to rush out.

"She told me she's had a crush on you for years," her teenage buddy piped in.

Oh, my! Kylee tried to pull her hand free, mortification tracing through her.

Chandler was beaming, and despite her embarrassment, all of her hopes of him someday noticing her like he had when they were teenagers blossomed. Was the superstar really staring at her as if she was appealing and his next date? But she selfishly didn't want to be just some date to him. She wanted to be the one for him. Like he'd always been the one for her.

She shook her head to try and clear it. The grown-up Chandler Delta was a huge player both on the field and off and she was too smart to let her heart get broken by the likes of him again. *Too late, you're drooling like he's a hot fudge sundae,* that snarky voice said.

Shut up, Mimi, she hurled back.

"Chandler," she leaned closer. "We have to talk."

"All right." He cocked his head. "Now?"

His teammate behind him called out, "Come on dude, let me flirt with the brunette now."

"Nope." Chandler shot his teammate a death glare. "She's mine."

Kylee should've protested. She wasn't any man's property, but Chandler claiming she was his made her out of breath and faint.

"Hey guys," Chandler said to her teenage buddies. "Help me out here?"

They both grinned. "Sure."

Chandler released her hand and Kylee felt the sting of disappointment. He'd been flirting with her just like he had the blonde and every other woman who flaunted themselves at him. She had to complete her mission, not let Chandler shuttle her off with the teenagers.

She started to tell him to wait, but he wasn't going anywhere. She was. The two young men next to her started manhandling her. Kylee cried out in surprise. The one boy took her legs and the other looped his hands under her armpits. They swept her off the ground and lifted her over the railing.

Kylee was about to tell them to stop, but strong hands reached up and she was lowered down and against the perfect, albeit sweaty, chest of one Chandler Delta, aka Superstar middie for the Boston Cannons and her lifelong crush. Time stopped as she stared into his blue eyes, so close, so appealing.

"Thanks guys," he told the boys.

"You're the best Chandler!" the one cried.

He tilted his chin to them as his arms were full of her. "Thank you," he told them.

Kylee heard a female voice, probably the blonde saying, "Why would he choose *her*?"

Her neck tightened at those words. Why would he indeed? The connection from when they were teenagers? She'd believed their kisses were unreal and their connection unparalleled, but she'd kissed a total of five different boys or men in her life, and none of them anywhere close to Chandler Delta's level of charm, so she didn't have a great comparison model. Could Chandler have felt the same about their bond and never forgotten her? That was asking for an impossible dream. Possibly he felt a little nostalgia for home and the memories of those fun summer times.

Or more likely ... Papa Delta had told his grandchildren to watch out for her and Chandler was instinctive enough to notice she looked like she'd been driving since yesterday and was running for her life and had information to convey before she was murdered. So he'd gotten her into his arms to protect her and pretend it was a romantic interest. That made sense.

She hated to look away from him, but she searched the stadium quickly, and thankfully did not see Creepy Eyes. But she could bet he was there, waiting her out. Would she endanger Chandler?

"I hate that I'm a sweaty mess the first time I get to hold you again in ten years." Chandler easily drew her attention back to him.

"You remember ... that?"

His blue gaze turned smoldering. "Beautiful Kylee ... I have never forgotten *that*."

Her entire body did a happy dance. She was lost in his blue eyes and the heady sensation of being held tight to his glorious body. She was in trouble. She was in a whole lot of trouble. She had no idea how to respond to his glorious proclamation, and her body was so hot she feared she'd combust.

Chandler turned and strode across the field and toward the locker rooms. Kylee wrapped her arms around his neck to hang on and was rewarded with one of his brilliant, irresistible smiles.

"I can't believe you came for me," he said. "Like a vision from heaven. Let me remedy the sweaty problem and then when we can really get reacquainted."

Kylee had no clue if he was intoning what she thought he was intoning. Would he kiss her again? It was probably wrong to indulge in such deliciousness when she needed to get the message sent and be back to running for her life, but kissing Chandler as full grown adults would be a memory she could take to the grave. Her superhero. Holding her in his arms. It was surreal.

She felt sadly that she had to set him straight about why she was here and get the information out as quickly as possible so she didn't spend too much time with him and put a target on his back. He was a Delta so she knew he had years of training, and an understanding of fighting, weapons, and subterfuge that was completely beyond her, but still that Creepy Eyes could shoot him in the back or something. She doubted her grandmother's flunky had any more idea of moral conduct than Mimi herself. Even worse if the man had been sent by King Frederick, the awful dictator who was trying to take over Europe and blustering that if

China or America tried to intervene it would be nuclear winter for their countries. Well she'd thought he was blustering until last night.

"Chandler," she whispered urgently.

"Yes, love?" He looked down at her with a beguiling smile as he strode across the field.

She tried valiantly to ignore the "love". He was a flirt and she would be smart not to lose her head. If only he wasn't her dream man.

"You know about the situation with my grandpa and the Delta secret?"

His gaze got serious. He walked to an overhang that was sheltered from view of the fans and relatively quiet, but he kept on holding her in his arms as if she weighed nothing. Impressive strength these lacrosse players had.

"Yes," he said. "Do you have information for me?"

She nodded. "I overheard something terrifying, now someone's following me, and my grandfather told me there's a price on my head."

"What?" he exclaimed. "Kylee." He held her even closer. "Let's get you somewhere safe."

She shook her head. "I'll disappear after I give you the info."

He gave her a challenging look that made her even more warm than his flirtatious ones. "I am not letting you out of my sight if you're in danger."

"Chandler," she tried.

"Don't," he warned. "I'll keep you safe. Where's your tail?"

She pushed out an exasperated breath, her safety was not the most important thing at the moment. She answered his question,

"I saw him as I was entering the stadium. He followed me from Chicago."

"Do you have a tracker on you?"

"I don't know." Her eyes widened. Could Mimi have put a tracker on her phone at some point, or dropped something in her purse when she wasn't looking? Her small purse was strapped across her chest. Should she ditch it?

"Okay. It's okay. Let's get inside, I'll hide you in the manager's office and we'll check your purse and phone for trackers before we sneak out of here." He gave her a smile that said he would enjoy the challenge of ditching her shadow. She only cared that he could accomplish such a deed. Was it wrong to let him protect her, to rely on him? Maybe, but she had no one else and no matter how she kidded herself she'd probably end up dead if she tried it on her own, and then she'd never see St. Lucia.

He started walking again as if it was all settled. She should've insisted she could stand on her own two feet but with as shaky and exhausted as she was Chandler carrying her was very, very nice.

Just like that she was lying to herself again. Like when she claimed she was five-two or she hadn't gained weight recently or she only ate ice cream on special occasions. Was it wrong to claim every day was a special occasion? Being in Chandler Delta's arms was definitely a special occasion, especially with his shirt off, even if he was sweaty and still had his chest protector on.

Chandler entered through a door. Suddenly there was a cacophony of noise and the shocking sight of men in various stages of undress.

"Oh!" Kylee cried out, burying her face in Chandler's warm skin.

"Sorry," he mumbled. "It's the only way to the office where you'll be safe. I didn't dare go through the stadium and have your tail follow or intercept us. Guys!" he called. "I've got an innocent beauty here. Cover up."

The men started whooping and yelling at them. Kylee heard all kinds of offers, many of which made her think she was much more innocent than Chandler could understand if he hung out with these men daily. She didn't understand men at all though, so maybe their language was normal for a men's locker room.

He strode quickly with her in his arms and she did not lift her head. He smelled of salt and sweat and amazingly it didn't offend her.

A door banged open and then closed and Chandler lowered her feet to the ground but kept his arm around her. "You okay?" he asked in a gravelly voice.

"Yes, thank you," her voice was too prim and she needed to lift her gaze from his muscles. He was over six feet so even with her heels she was eye level with his glorious chest.

She forced herself to raise her gaze, and got lost in those blue eyes of his. She knew all the Deltas had those incredible eyes, but Chandler's had always seemed more intriguing to her than any of the other family members. They had the power to make her forget everything but wanting to be closer to her. Hypnotic eyes.

"You'll be safe here. Security won't let anyone into the locker room. I'll hurry and shower and then we'll de-bug you and make a plan." He gave her a winning smile, released her from his arms, and hurried out of the office, shutting the door behind him. Luckily the window had drawn blinds over it so she couldn't see what might be happening out in that locker room.

She sat heavily in a hard chair and took slow breaths, hoping to calm her racing pulse as she fingered her jade necklace. Touching it usually calmed her but not right now.

Chandler Delta. Holding her close. Claiming he would protect her. Her mind starting racing with visions of the two of them on the run, him sheltering her, being her hero, stealing kisses any chance he got.

The office was suddenly sweltering hot. She fanned herself and made a firm promise. No ice cream tonight and no romance novel reading time.

She burst out laughing at herself and wondered if she was going insane. Tonight she might be dead or hidden away in a closet for her own protection. She might never eat ice cream or read a romance again.

She bit at her lip. But she might spend more time with Chandler Delta. He was more appetizing than romance novels or ice cream. And that was saying a lot.

Find Endangered on Amazon.

Also by Cami Checketts

Delta Family Romances

Deceived

Abandoned

Committed

Betrayed

Devoted

Compromised

Endangered

Accepted

Returned

Devastated

Famous Friends Romances

Loving the Firefighter

Loving the Athlete

Loving the Rancher

Loving the Coach

Loving the Contractor

Loving the Sheriff

Loving the Entertainer

The Hidden Kingdom Romances

Royal Secrets

Only Her Undercover Spy

Only Her Cowboy

Only Her Best Friend

Only Her Blue-Collar Billionaire

Only Her Injured Stuntman

Only Her Amnesiac Fake Fiancé

Only Her Hockey Legend

Only Her Smokejumper Firefighter

Only Her Christmas Miracle

Jewel Family Romance

Do Marry Your Billionaire Boss

Do Trust Your Special Ops Bodyguard

Do Date Your Handsome Rival

Do Rely on Your Protector

Do Kiss the Superstar

Do Tease the Charming Billionaire

Do Claim the Tempting Athlete

Do Depend on Your Keeper

Strong Family Romance

Don't Date Your Brother's Best Friend

Her Loyal Protector

Don't Fall for a Fugitive

Her Hockey Superstar Fake Fiance

Don't Ditch a Detective

Caribbean Rescue

Cozumel Escape

Cancun Getaway

Trusting the Billionaire

How to Kiss a Billionaire

Onboard for Love

Shadows in the Curtain

Billionaire Bride Pact Romance

The Resilient One

The Feisty One

The Independent One

The Protective One

The Faithful One

The Daring One

Park City Firefighter Romance

Rescued by Love

Reluctant Rescue

Stone Cold Sparks

Snowed-In for Christmas

Echo Ridge Romance

Christmas Makeover

Last of the Gentlemen

My Best Man's Wedding

Change of Plans

Counterfeit Date

Snow Valley

Full Court Devotion: Christmas in Snow Valley

A Touch of Love: Summer in Snow Valley

Running from the Cowboy: Spring in Snow Valley

Light in Your Eyes: Winter in Snow Valley

Romancing the Singer: Return to Snow Valley

Fighting for Love: Return to Snow Valley

Other Books by Cami

Seeking Mr. Debonair: Jane Austen Pact

Seeking Mr. Dependable: Jane Austen Pact

Saving Sycamore Bay

Oh, Come On, Be Faithful

Protect This

Blog This

Redeem This

The Broken Path

Dead Running

Dying to Run

Fourth of July

Love & Loss

Love & Lies

About the Author

Cami is a part-time author, part-time exercise consultant, part-time housekeeper, full-time wife, and overtime mother of four adorable boys. Sleep and relaxation are fond memories. She's never been happier.

Join Cami's VIP list to find out about special deals, giveaways and new releases and receive a free copy of *Rescued by Love: Park City Firefighter Romance* by clicking here.

cami@camichecketts.com

www.camichecketts.com

Made in United States
Orlando, FL
30 March 2023

31546535R00130